I haven't left hearth and home and trekked into the wilderness, not yet, but novelist Michael Connelly and *Mountain Lyrics* made me feel as if I had.

Mountain Lyrics author invites the reader to look to *Midsummer Night's Dream* for resonance. The link is apt, not only in the way Connelly weaves complexities of plot and subplot so compellingly, but also in his dream-like setting and character set that were anything but ordinary. Connelly's enchanted forest is the Big Rock Candy Mountain, a hobo's vision of utopia. Connelly's mountain is a place part escapist dreamscape and part all-too-real hardship.

Buck and Bob-a-Lou, a donkey purchased for the trip into the wilderness, cross paths with a screwball cast of characters: Mac and Lucky, Jesse and Sister Toni, and Moses McLaren. No predictable folks here. Okay, maybe the donkey, but nobody else. Each of them has a story to tell that takes them from a star shrouded valley to the mountain's summit and beyond. Oh, and the bear. A quest for courage should have a bear.

Buck's journey, and ours with him, are worth taking.

Mike Donohue

Like reading a secret message from my soul. Whether a Rock Candy Mountain or a simple longing for essence and hope, Mike gave this reader a story to take home at the end of a long day.

Jerome Leveque

A story told with humor, an engaging sense of self-deprecation, and an affinity for his subject, Mike Connelly writes a poem in prose form. This is a page turner as Buck's vision quest takes him to places he's never known existed—inside himself. A must read.

Milt Rowland

Mountain Lyrics

A Quest For Courage

Michael F. Connelly

Published by:
Gray Dog Press
Spokane, Washington
www.GrayDogPress.com

Printed in the United States

ISBN: 978-1-936178-11-7

Library of Congress Control Number: 2010925335

Artwork: Gabriel Brown

This book is dedicated to my family.
They make me complete.

ACKNOWLEDGEMENTS

I would like to express my gratitude to the
many friends and colleagues who provided me
with pointed and sometimes painful advice.
Special thanks to Erik Lamb and Jandon
Mitchell for their exacting editing and
enthusiastic support and
Gabriel Brown for his brilliant artwork.

INTRODUCTION

Most of us slip quietly through life afraid to hear the promptings of our hearts.

Our modern world encourages this, insulating us from the howl of fierce winds and the embrace of vast empty spaces, robbing us of our courage.

At times we seek comfort by befriending those who complement our careful constructs and for a time we share a tentative state of ease, bolstered by our assumption that our companions see and touch the world in the same way we do.

That isn't how it works.

In truth, we share little. We are islands of feelings and fears that move together for a time in the same direction. It is our instinctive recognition of this separation that makes us hesitant to reach too deeply into life's waters. We know we are reaching into those waters alone.

I remember a book I read when I was in the fourth grade. It was suggested by my teacher, Sister Antonio, a formidable, attractive nun. The book was about a boy who prayed for adventure and God gave it to him. He was trapped in a car trunk, overheard bad guys say bad things and after a number of fearful events, got away and crawled back into his own bed. The point of the book was that we don't need adventure; we just need to appreciate being home, safe and sound in the comforting presence of God. Well, the boy did mouth the words and swore he would never utter such a prayer again. But I've never believed he meant it. I figured he'd rather be out having an adventure.

Mountain Lyrics is an adventure shared by a number of people who find a way to reach into those fearful currents, listen to the promptings of their hearts, and, just for a moment, touch the glory of God.

When I finished this manuscript and asked my family to read it, my daughter asked which character was me. My response was all of them, one way or another.

In the Big Rock Candy Mountains there's a land
    that's fair and bright.
Where the handouts grow on bushes and you
    sleep out every night.
Where the boxcars all are empty and the sun
    shines every day
On the birds and the bees and the cigarette
    trees,
The lemonade springs where the bluebird sings,
In the Big Rock Candy Mountains.

An excerpt from The Big Rock Candy Mountain,
Author Unknown

The Rock Candy Mountain

Moses McClaren's

All Met

Sister Toni's

Shot Rang Out

gabriel brown

CHAPTER ONE

Four days will quickly steep
Themselves in nights
Four nights will quickly dream away the time
And then the moon, like to a silverbow
New-bent in heaven, shall behold the night
Of our solemnities. ₁

Buck had fallen asleep when the deep bellow of a tractor horn burst in his head and headlights exploded into his eyes. He reared back in terror, smashing the back of his balding head against the stock of the LC Smith mounted behind him. Frantically, he yanked the hard plastic steering wheel to the right then back to the left, trying to avoid the hurtling semi that had appeared directly in his path. His tires were screaming, the donkey was screaming and

Buck was screaming as his truck and trailer skidded out of control.

Buck dynamited his brakes. The truck's wheels locked up and the back end of his pick-up began to slide towards the right side of the road. In his mirror, he caught a glimpse of his trailer swinging back in the opposite direction. Ahead the truck's yellow lights sliced through dark layers of fog.

Fighting to gain control, Buck turned into the skid. He released then pumped his brakes, holding the steering wheel pinned to the right, struggling to keep his rig on the roadway. Abruptly, Buck felt his tires dig into soft gravel. For an instant, the driver's side of the truck lifted and then settled as Buck wrestled with the wheel, trying to steer a straight path down the side of the highway.

The deep gravel pulled at Buck's tires and the truck slowed. He could feel the weight of the trailer pushing behind him. Finally, he was able to bring the truck to a stop.

Buck gripped the steering wheel, his pounding heart and shaking hands the only remnant of the noise and turmoil of the past few seconds. He carefully reached back to touch the spot where his head had smashed into the shotgun. He felt a lump, tender and beginning to swell. He couldn't tell by his touch if he was bleeding or not. His right foot trembled on the brake pedal. The acrid scent of burnt rubber filled the cab. He brought his hand forward and glanced at his fingers in the weak dash light.

"Well, no blood anyway, son of a bitch."

For a minute, he felt like throwing up but after a few deep breaths his stomach settled. Then out of nowhere he found himself giggling. Giggling and sniffing and taking a deep breath that ended with a gasp then a sob.

"Fucking A."

Buck shook his head and wiped the tears from his eyes. As he took another ragged breath, he heard the donkey sounding off.

"Goddamn donkey. That was one of my better ideas."

Buck switched off the engine and headlights then opened the truck door and stepped outside. For a moment he was unnerved by the darkness and the sudden silence. He stood quietly while the damp night air swirled gently around him, touching his face and hands. He began to inch his way down the side of the pick-up bed. The metal was damp and cold to his touch. His legs were still shaky. Finally, he reached the trailer and popped down a side window. He had just reached inside and grabbed a handful of grain when the donkey stuck her hot wet lips into his ear and brayed. Buck jumped and shouted out.

"Jesus donkey!"

He wiped his ear with one hand and held the grain to the donkey's mouth with the other. Bob-a-Lou slurped and chewed, grabbing at Buck's fingers when the grain was gone.

Buck clicked on the trailer's light switch located on the roof to the right of the window then walked around to the back gate, opened it and stepped into the trailer, latching the gate behind him.

The donkey nuzzled him, pushing her nose into his chest and then danced away when Buck touched her flank. He knelt down next to the donkey and carefully ran his hands over her torso then down each leg. Bob-a-Lou jumped a little at each touch. He spoke to her quietly, "Don't seem any worse for wear, old girl." He was surprised that the donkey was not injured. As he rubbed the base of the donkey's ears Bob-a-Lou quieted.

Buck reached forward and pressed the lever that poured water into a dish built into the side of the trailer then crawled out, kicking the straw and donkey shit off his knees and boots. He latched the back gate. Walking back to the side window, he turned off the light and locked the window down.

"We'll be there soon Bob-a-Lou," Buck said to the restless hoofs just inside. "Hang in there."

A car passed, lights then sound, both fading as the car continued down the hill and out of sight.

Buck leaned back against the side of his truck. Thin layers of clouds hung suspended just above the ground, diminishing the faint light from the night sky. His thoughts began to drift from the chaos of the near collision to the reason for his presence on this particular mountain pass in the first place.

At first he'd just been looking for empty spaces on a map of Montana, looking for a place to get away. Then he found a valley that ran from mid-state to the Canadian border with few roads and fewer people. The valley was ringed by mountains and peaks with names and legends that could have been lifted from a poem by Robert Service. He found himself filled by a desire to go into that valley, but at the same time experienced a fleeting sense of foreboding, a tickle of fear about traveling alone in a place so unfamiliar. He was reluctant to cross that line between his well-ordered dreams of adventure and the uncertain reality of entering the woods. The whole thing gnawed at him, right in the center of his belly.

He remembered talking to his wife about the trip but she had appeared to be more concerned about him quitting his job with no inclination to get another. He figured she'd lumped all this "back to the woods stuff" in with the general craziness he'd exhibited over the last several months. She didn't understand what was driving him. He didn't understand what was driving him either.

Buck recalled his wife's attempt at levity when he was loading the truck, when he had finally decided to risk pursuing his uncertain desire. "Don't get eaten by a grizzly," she had said, smiling, then turned away and headed for the house. She might have been a little pissed, maybe scared, he didn't ask. "I don't plan on dying," he had called to her retreating back. She stopped on the porch and turned back towards him, looking at him as if she had a question to ask but was reluctant to do so. Then without speaking, she opened the door and stepped inside and he had hit the road. When he turned onto the highway his trailer was rattling, the donkey was braying and inexplicably he felt pretty good.

Now, as Buck leaned back against the cold metal of the truck, he thought again about their parting, realizing that her unspoken concern was just one more thing left unsaid. One more piece of the full and confusing space that had come to separate them. Buck thought about times, now long past, when they had both been convinced that nothing could ever come between them. He smiled at that, wondering if it was still true, remembering the days when all he had to do was reach out with one hand and they would be together, touching each other, not needing to say anything at all. Buck would get so lost in those moments that he would forget what he was doing or sometimes even where he was. When he came up for air he'd have to look around and take some time to figure things out.

◆ ◆ ◆ ◆

Buck could still recall the very day that state of confusion began. It was almost thirty years ago. Winter had ended. Snowmelt from the empty hills was tearing recklessly down the ravines and draws of the foothills. New life, lush and verdant, exploded from every crevice and available patch of earth, gorging on the abundant new waters and reaching upwards towards the warmth of the spring sun. Buck was sitting on a rock ledge overlooking this explosion of spring and the faded structures of the town below. Melinda was sitting right beside him. Their feet were hanging in the air above the wide-leafed blackberries that filled the bottom of the cut.

Buck was still winded from the climb. He could feel the sweat on his back cooling in the breeze that drifted down the hillside. Melinda was quiet, swinging her legs, occasionally looking over at him. He watched as she raised her face to the chilled air then deftly rolled her hair up onto her head. He could see the moisture glistening on the back of her neck.

Hesitantly, Buck reached out and laid his hand next to hers on the broken granite. Melinda was still, her eyes now on Buck's hand as it rested beside her.

Buck slowly moved his fingers over her fingers, gradually entwining her hand with his own, feeling her grasp tighten in response to his. She looked up at him, her eyes wide, questioning, her mouth partly open. He could see her chest rise and fall as she took a deep breath and then slowly exhaled, her eyes never losing contact with his. Oh sweet Jesus, he thought, almost uttering the words out loud. Her hand was cold but electric; he could feel his own heart pounding. The sensation was at first so intense that he looked down, afraid to continue to look into her eyes.

The two of them sat on the side of the ravine, holding hands and quietly talking as the sun set and the night sky settled around them. Finally Buck helped Melinda up and they walked down the rough path to the valley below. They could hear the sudden cries of predator and prey and the distant sounds of the city. Melinda walked close, her hand lightly resting on the small of his back.

At the bottom of the hill they sat together on a wooden bench near the Clearwater, watching the river's smooth waters reflect the stars as they slowly appeared, listening to its rush and splash, just being together, their lives ahead but not pressing, not yet.

◆ ◆ ◆ ◆

It was getting colder. Buck stepped away from the truck, rubbing his arms with chilled hands. He had half a mind to hop in his truck, cross the highway and hightail it back to Melinda, to his home. He wanted to sit close to her and feel the warmth of her breath and talk. Talk to her about the memories that had, for the first time in too long, filled his imagination. But even as he formed the idea of returning, he put it aside. It didn't feel right. His yearning to recapture those past moments and his compulsion to visit the valley that lay before him were mixed together somehow, two parts of the same thing. He leaned his head back against the cab and looked up through the thinning and broken cover at the stars that filled the sky from horizon to horizon. Taking a deep breath he inhaled the exotic scent of damp wood and evergreen needles and water falling someplace near, wondering what the hell he was doing and knowing that he was here for a reason, all at the same time.

Suddenly Buck heard the sound of branches breaking. Frightened, he quickly hoisted himself into the cab, slamming the door shut behind him. He started up the truck and turned on the headlights, trying to identify what spooked him. He could see nothing in the dim reach of his lights but the empty road ahead. He switched on the heater, stretching his feet past the pedals and gingerly leaned back. He took one more deep breath in, and then out.

Buck listened to the rumble of the truck's engine and realized that he didn't really feel like going anywhere. Bob-a-Lou seemed okay, whatever had spooked him was gone and he had no desire to either continue or turn around. So he settled into his seat and did nothing. As he relaxed, his head against the cold window, the blow from the heater hot and soothing, a memory nudged at him. At first he couldn't quite grasp it but then he remembered; it was years ago, eighty pounds ago, lots of dollars under the bridge ago...

He was in northern Canada and had just picked up a message at an old and barely open general store in Juniper B.C. The hand scrawled note advised him that his ride home had taken another route. "Sorry." Juniper was one of those towns where the highway slides through without much of an interruption. Dust from the store parking lot scaled across the roadway's uneven asphalt and came to rest on the wooden steps of an empty hotel on the other side of the highway. At 8:00 in the morning it was warm enough that his shirt stuck to his sides. He had woken that morning intending to have a hot meal then continue down the highway, heading home. When he realized that he had lost his wallet, his sense of purpose began to fade. Looking for it, he frantically tossed and unpacked his gear and found nothing. After he spent the last of his pocket change for a Coke his sense of purpose was gone. No ride, no money, go back, go forward, he didn't know. He had planned on hitting his ride up for a loan but that wasn't going to work. He walked to the side of the highway and stuck out his thumb, heading south, a long ride with no money. Before the first car came he pulled back his hand and after the car rushed by in a cloud of dust he crossed the highway and stuck out his thumb heading in the opposite direction, back to the camp where he'd spent the last month. The camp was closer but that didn't feel right either and after one car passed without slowing he crossed the road again. He was hungry, in a strange place, a bit over eighteen years of age and just didn't know what to do.

Well, I guess I've come full circle, he thought. The only thing different now was his age and his increasing tendency to worry about most everything. For most of those years between, he'd always had projects to complete, bills to pay, and kids to worry over. He'd been driven with purpose from the time he got up each morning, even if it was just to go fishing or travel two hundred miles to watch a kid play ball. As the house emptied and the job started looking the same each and every day he found that getting up in the morning was harder. Little things, things he would have handled in his sleep five years ago had begun to trouble him. Problems at work or with money would cause him to lie awake at night, sometimes mumbling the Lord's Prayer under his breath in an attempt to push back the willies and fall asleep, mumbling away and worrying and not believing, really, that the words were going to help. Not believing that anything was going to get much better any time soon.

He considered turning on the radio and decided not to, and then he remembered, it was broke. He spent a little time thinking about fixing it. One of the wires was shorted or loose or disconnected somehow. Adjusting his position, he turned off the headlights, fiddled with the steering wheel and thought about the job he had left. He remembered packing ten years of ideas, good and bad, case studies he had toyed with and never finished and cards and mementos he'd kept, old toys. He smiled as he thought of laughing out loud about the mayor's last speech with one of his lawyers, laughing, secure and comfortable with the knowledge that they knew how things worked and the mayor didn't have a clue. A good clean laugh behind closed doors in his sanctuary built with years of hard work and anxious moments. The sanctuary he'd walked away from.

Warmed by the truck heater, Buck fell asleep wondering if he was more likely to be poisoned by carbon monoxide with the window closed or cracked.

He woke in the dark with the same thought that had put him to sleep and glanced at the closed window. Alive, but unsure what woke him, he stretched, pushing his feet against the floorboards, then started, catching sight of something moving to the right of the truck. Buck sat forward and peered out the window but couldn't see anything. He hesitated for a minute then slowly opened the truck's door and stepped down onto the gravel. He could hear the donkey shift in the trailer. Buck thought about the shotgun then decided against it. He closed the door quietly behind him and stood still, listening. He could feel his heart beating; could hear the rasp of his breath sliding in and out and the sound of the donkey shuffling. Finally, he relaxed. He figured it was just an elk or deer. He turned to get back into the cab and suddenly felt the cold touch of metal press firmly up against his ear.

"Put your fuckin' hands on top of the cab, cowboy."

The voice was right beside Buck, coming out of nowhere. Buck placed both hands on the cab. "Okay, okay, what the hell is this?" Buck could smell alcohol, sweet and slightly rotting and the smell made his heart race with fear more than the gun pressed against his head.

"What do you want?" Buck's legs were shaking, his hands cold on the roof of the cab.

"Shut up and don't move." Whoever it was leaned closer, overwhelming him with the odor of rank sweat and tequila. Buck leaned closer to the cab, his thoughts filled with the white roar of panic.

"Hey Mac!"

Buck heard another voice then the sound of the trailer gate creaking open. Oh shit, he thought, the donkey, he'd just gotten the damn donkey and these guys were going to take it.

His wife was going to love this.

"Goddamn it!" Buck heard a clump and the sound of someone scuffling, then Bob-a-Lou's bray followed by more clumps. A hoarse, strained voice from behind the trailer cried out, "The mule whacked out. I'm not going in there again. It kicked me in the nuts, you come get it."

"I can't get it you idiot, I'm holding the gun." To emphasize this Mac poked Buck in the ear.

"Ow! Damn!" Buck exclaimed.

"Oh, sorry man," Mac responded.

Buck, his heart slowing, felt the barrel of the gun pull back a little and thought, incredulously, sorry man? What the hell was going on? Buck carefully turned a little more towards his assailant. The gun barrel was back a foot or so from his head. Mac was looking towards the back of the trailer where the light from a flashlight was wiggling around, lighting up random pieces of tree and rock.

"Come on you butt-head we gotta get the mule and get out of here," Mac shouted.

"No way, no way Mac, I'm hurtin'. Have the guy get the mule."

Mac paused and looked back at Buck, "Yeah. Okay, get the mule," he ordered and pushed the barrel back towards Buck's head.

"She's not a mule," Buck muttered.

"What?"

"She's a donkey."

"I don't give a rat's ass what she is, just get it goddamnit!" Mac boomed, spraying spit everywhere and waving the gun erratically.

Buck watched the barrel and Mac both dancing a little weave as Mac yelled.

Mac's partner came around from the back of the trailer, the light from his flash still jumping all over.

Buck turned slowly and faced Mac. "You want me to unload the donkey?"

"That's the ticket boyo." The barrel jerked towards him again. It seemed a pretty timid jerk to Buck. Shaking his head, not quite sure whether he should be afraid of these dingdongs or just walk away, Buck moved to the back of the trailer and Mac and his partner followed. The back gate was open, the beam from the flashlight glanced off of Bob-a-Lou's gray coat and the trees then blinded Buck as it swept over his face.

Buck reached inside the door and clicked on the trailer light. In the sudden glare, Buck could see Mac's round face and gray unkempt whiskers appear out of the darkness. His eyes were wide open, his nose large and veined. A stained and torn Carhart was wrapped tightly around his barrel stomach. His shotgun was held high in his right hand. Mac's partner was caught in the same snapshot. He had a slighter build and wore a torn heavy wool sweater, soiled and dingy. His lean, younger face was covered by a day or two's growth of red beard. Both wore wide-brimmed oilskin hats that were dark and misshapen.

Panicked, they stepped back from the light, steps synchronized, shouting, guns swinging up above their heads.

"Hey! Shit! What are you doing? Goddamn it! I can't see!"

Buck hesitated then ignored their shouts and bent down and stepped into the trailer. He could feel his heart slowing, less certain that he would come to any harm. He grabbed Bob-a-Lou's harness and fitted it over the donkey's ears, eased by the smell and feel of the donkey's rough coat and warm wet breath. The shouting outside ended and Buck could hear one of them coming towards the trailer.

"Come on girl."

He slowly turned the animal inside the trailer and stepped it down off the trailer bed, looping the reins on the door handle. Mac cautiously approached the open trailer and looked inside. Seeing Buck's gear, he whistled and gestured with the barrel again.

"Fuckin' gold mine, load 'er up."

Goddamn, all my stuff, never even used, Buck thought. He lifted the heavy wool blanket and full leather side packs from the trailer hooks. His .44 was tucked, unloaded, in one side of the trail pack and all his ammo was in the other. His shotgun was in the cab. Buck hoped they wouldn't look in the cab. In the light from the trailer's open door he methodically smoothed the blanket over the back of the donkey and threw on the trail packs, reaching under the donkey for the cinch to pull it tight. Bob-a-Lou shuffled sideways and swelled her gut, blowing out as Buck gently kneed her. "That's okay old girl, loosen up, there we go." Buck fussed with her, scratching her ears, wondering if he would ever see the donkey again.

Buck turned towards Mac. In that instant, just behind Mac, Buck saw the younger man's hat fly off of his head and a small fountain of blood spring upward like a geyser. At the same time he heard the sharp retort and whine of a carbine. The redhead was falling backwards out of the light. Mac and Buck froze, staring at each other. Mac screamed, "Get into the woods!" Buck grabbed the reins and stumbled down the ditch on the side of the road, dragging Bob-a-Lou. He glanced back and saw Mac bend down and effortlessly pick up his partner then jump off the road behind him. Two more shots rang out and Buck ran into the darkness, plants and tree limbs tearing at his legs and swatting him in the face. He could hear Mac crashing through the forest beside him. The donkey was sounding off and pulling back. Buck stepped on and over a moss covered rock then took another step out into open air. The last thing he remembered was Bob-a-Lou pulling the reins from his hands and falling slowly into blackness.

CHAPTER TWO

Thou remembrest
Since once I sat upon a promontory
And heard a mermaid on a dolphin's back
Uttering such dulcet and harmonious breath
That the rude sea grew civil at her song
And certain stars shot madly from their spheres
To hear the sea-maid's music. 2

Sister Toni was hauling fresh water to a pair of young lambs thrown off by their mother and an old ewe that looked like it was ready to drop. Though it grew harder every year, she still made the effort to carry two five-gallon buckets at a time. As she approached the barn she could feel her arthritic fingers freezing and stiffening around the thin metal handles. Setting the damp buckets into their wooden stand, she painfully opened her hands and then turned and stood surveying the valley that was her home. Her thin shoulders were held back and rigid as she slowly rubbed her hands together, patiently working the pain away.

The meadow before her appeared as a dark slope rolling downhill from where she stood, surrounded by the blackened borders of trees and mountains, the tops of the hills dark in contrast with the lighter shade of the evening sky. The chill air was still touched by the scent of sun-warmed hay left from last week's cutting. High above, the trees and rocky peaks of the mountain were framed by stars so thick it seemed that God had thrown handfuls out in every direction.

The sight caused Toni to feel small and of little importance but she took some comfort in it nevertheless. She knew, surely knew, that God held her that very moment in the hollow of His hand and that she in turn held the lambs and ewes and the young children, whose thin and clear voices sang to her from across the meadow, in the hollow of her own hands. The children were singing the moon song, singing to a cold moon that was hiding tonight, singing the song taught to them by their newest visitor, a young girl who had appeared seven days ago, a gaunt and fearful bundle of dark eyes and pale skin. Big dark eyes that Toni had seen sparkle too few times since her arrival.

I see the moon
The moon sees me
The moon sees the one
I long to see.

Listening to the children's voices, Toni thought of ones she had longed to see, smiling as she thought back over the years, wondering if she ever had longed to see anyone. If she did, he must not have made much of an impression, she thought.

When she thought of her youth her memories of boys were more often marked by anger and confusion than anything else. She wasn't social or popular in high school. Any inclination she had to join a group or club was short lived if present at all. She didn't remember herself as being attractive; the boys would usually ignore her, sometimes talking about her as she walked past, occasionally ridiculing her in front of others.

She was poor. She didn't wear anything but long skirts and full blouses and had only a few of each. She remembered one time when she was standing in front of a poster announcing that cheerleader tryouts would take place the following week. She was just looking, trying to imagine what it would be like to be a cheerleader. Suddenly one of the football players came up behind her and lifted her up from the waist.

He held her up in the air and chanted some football idiocy as she struggled and turned beet red. She never forgot her embarrassment when she had turned away from the crowd of laughing students that greeted her as she was set down. Nor had she forgotten the boy's touch, the heat and surprising strength of his hands, his casual invasion of her self. Her senses had been awakened, her thoughts filled with equal parts of panic and desire, all of it coalescing into an aching and profound sense of shame and humiliation.

At the beginning of her senior year, Toni realized that she had become accustomed to the quiet and solitude of the near empty pews during morning mass. Her presence and observance had evolved into something very personal, almost intimate; it seemed to set her apart.

As the priest performed the sacrament without an audience, just he and God and the careful exercise of ancient rites, Toni felt part of a timeless truth, the unique and unprecedented discourse between God and man. When she knelt during the lengthy consecration and the litany that accompanied it she found that she welcomed the discomfort of her sore knees and aching back. It helped her to set aside the meaningless and trivial worries of the day that awaited her and allowed her to focus her thoughts on God, to wait patiently for a connection, a response, something to fill the emptiness inside of her. And at times she would have glimpses of what she thought was God's presence. A sudden shudder from His touch would cut to her core and then be gone. Its absence more telling than its momentary hereness. It seemed that her faith grew more out of recognition of what was missing then a present sense of His being. It was that emptiness and the hope that it would, on occasion, be filled that carried her through her subsequent schooling and vows.

Finally, the day came when she was to choose her specific vocation. She was prompted to sign up to work at a convent in the middle of nowhere to help kids that had no place left to go, prompted by a flier with a picture of a lush green valley and two young children holding hands. She knew as soon as she looked at the picture that they were to be her children and that the valley was to be her home. So she had come to this wilderness and found God in the cold waters, fierce storms and warm fragrant afternoons and it filled her up, all of it, and she had felt joy for the first time.

That was a long time ago, Toni thought, as she stood quietly in her surroundings listening to the children's song. She explored for a moment her current state of joy and experienced a brief pang of regret for a course of life that she had never chosen, never allowed to touch her. Then shaking her head she started back, walking purposely, chiding herself for her weakness, and forced her thoughts to the present, to Jesse, her newest ward.

Toni had found Jesse in the same manner the pharaoh's daughter had found the child Moses, asleep in the reeds by the lake. She had been wrapped in an old Pendleton blanket, her head resting on a torn backpack, her hand clutching an open knife. Sister Toni had stood back, not wanting to startle her, and called out softly, "Child, are you not well?" Jesse woke, jerking back and away from her then jumped up holding the knife in one hand and her pack in the other, the blanket falling at her feet.

"Stay away!" Jesse hissed, bent over like an old witch, holding the knife out in front of her.

"You have nothing to fear here," Sister Toni whispered.

Then as she watched Jesse slowly lower the knife, she softly said, "I have food," and continued, "There is shelter just over the hill," gesturing to her right, across the valley.

She saw that her words and perhaps her outfit, a nun's habit without that ridiculous headpiece, were beginning to soothe the girl so she stayed and talked softly for a long time.

Now Jesse was here, and was sad, deep down in her heart, and Sister Toni was troubled and patiently waiting for God to help her ease Jesse's pain.

God bless the moon
And God bless me
And God bless the one
I long to see.

The singing stopped and Toni completed her walk, stepping carefully down the darkened path to the cluster of buildings that was her home. The other two sisters, both older, had already gone to bed. She heard the children begging Jesse for a story. When she pulled open the door to the bunkhouse she saw three young children, two girls and a boy, leaning out of their bunks, Jesse sitting on the floor between them. The light from the kerosene lantern was flickering on their faces as Jesse, in a soft sing-song voice, told her story. Her hands, it seemed by their own volition, rose to accompany the telling.

Once upon a time, a long time ago, there was a man named Bill Bungle. He had two children, Jill and little Bill, and a great big dog named King. They lived in a valley in the mountains that was surrounded by high snowy peaks. The valley was nestled up against a very unusual mountain of blue and green rocks, tall trees, and springs that splashed and gurgled from rock to rock. The mountain was

25

called the Big Rock Candy Mountain. Every morning the wind, fragrant with the scent of pine and cedar, would slip down from the mountain waking everything it touched. The flowers on the ground would slowly unbend and stand straight, the lake would begin to move and reach out to touch the sand on the beach and a smile would appear on the face of every single child.

Sister Toni could see Jesse smile, a smile that lit up Jesse's whole face, and then in response she saw a smile form on each child's face, faces filled with delight, anticipating the story to come. Jesse, her hands gracefully tracing the path of the wind, continued:

Every evening the wind blew from the lake back to the mountains. The waters became still. The flowers closed and drooped, grasses would lie down and the children rested their heads on pillows and slept with dreams of narrow paths and soft thick moss and clear blue pools 'neath the soft fall of water. In the dark of night the mountain would speak, calling to all children with kind hearts or restless souls.

One morning, just before dawn, before the winds began to flow, Jill woke. She pulled on her sweater and pants and ran barefoot out the door onto the porch, then around the back of the cabin to a path that led up the mountain. She had woken with a singular memory, an old tale that her mother had told her years ago. Her Mom had told her that near the top of the mountain, where the path turns around the huge boulder and dips below a hollow tree, at the moment the sun climbs above the mountain peaks, a door would open and through the door a wondrous valley would appear. A drink of the water of the stream in that valley would heal all hurts and ease all fears. Jill needed that water. Their dog King had come home ill the night before and she was afraid that without this magic potion he wouldn't heal. Bill Bungle had done what he could but had shaken his head of curly gray hair and looked at little Bill and Jill and said, "It doesn't look good kids, but we'll let him rest easy tonight." Then Bill Bungle gently laid King next to the fireplace. King's breath was quick and shallow. As he lay on his side, King looked directly at Jill with his large yellow eyes and Jill could have sworn that she heard him say, "You can help me."

And that was exactly what Jill planned to do.

Jill had no light, but she followed the dark line between the tall shadows of the trees and rocks as it twisted and turned up the mountain. Once she walked around a large boulder and stopped, realizing that she no longer could see where to go. The surface of the rock was smooth and wet underneath her left hand. As she walked around the rock all she could see were shadows of trees and fog and darkness. She was getting cold and was afraid. She'd lost her way. Suddenly she was startled by a throaty warble. The dark shape of a turkey hightailed away from the rock then slowed and bent awkwardly to peck here and there at the ground. Curious, Jill stepped toward the bobbing bird and realized that the path, draped in fog and dark, was once again before her. "Well thank you Mr. Turkey!" she told the turkey's back as it disappeared from view to the left of the path. She continued on her way, hurrying now, because she knew she had to reach the top before the sun came up.

After stumbling up the path, Jill came to a spot where a massive stone, split in two pieces, seemed to block her way. In the first early light of the morning she could see that a narrow dirt path wound its way between the two halves of granite. On the other side of this cut she could see the top of the mountain, a pile of large boulders broken only by the shadows of dwarf alpine trees. She walked carefully between the stones but the path abruptly ended at the base of a huge boulder that rested against an ancient pine tree. The top of the pine tree had been blown off, probably by lightning, Jill thought. The tree's trunk was burnt and hollow.

No door or opening of any kind could be seen.

Jill sat down, right in the dirt at the end of the path, tired and disappointed. Suddenly, as the sun peeked over the mountains to the east, a single ray leaped out from the horizon and touched the jumbled rocks in front of her. She realized that what she'd thought was a shadow on the stone was actually a gap. She hurried to the small opening and squeezed inside. Walking as quickly as she could, her hands braced on the cold walls of the rock on either side, she headed upward. She followed this new path as it twisted abruptly to the right then left and found herself standing at the edge of a steep slope. In front of her was a small narrow valley set deeply within sheer rock cliffs and covered with green grasses. The valley was split right down the middle by a *stream fed by waters pouring from the rocks to her right.*

Jill quickly pulled out a pewter flask and filled it with the falling water, capped it, and turned back into the fissure. All she could think of now was King and getting back to the cabin on time. Emerging from the stone she ran down the path, now well lit with the morning sun, and didn't stop until their cabin came into view.

Exhausted, taking big breaths, Jill ran up the worn wooden steps to the porch and pulled open the door.

"Dad! Dad! Bill! Get up, get up!" She yelled as she fell to her knees in front of King, who was still lying in front of the fire. She leaned down and placed her ear against King's side.

Jesse reached up and pulled one of the little girls into her lap, pressing the child's head to her chest. Sister Toni, tears in her eyes, pressed her twisted hand to her own chest reaching for the pulse of her heart, as Jesse continued:

"Jill listened and listened…"

And the little girl cried out, her small ear pressed into Jesse's bosom, "I hear it, I hear King's heart."

"And alive he was, just barely." Jesse said, drawing out the words.

Sister Toni stood quietly, watching and listening as she felt her own heart pushing back against her open hand.

Jill, now surrounded by Bill Bungle and little Bill, held up King's head and dribbled the water from the flask into his mouth. King was still as death, then suddenly his tongue reached out and licked his lips to lap up the water. Jill quickly poured the water from the flask into a tin and King lifted his head and lapped that up too then slowly struggled to his feet. Jill buried her face in King's gray and brown fur.

"He's okay, he's okay."

And he was and would be for a very long time to come.

Jesse finished, spent, with the little girl in her lap. Sister Toni lifted the little girl and laid her into bed.

"Now cover your heads and close your eyes for daylight comes early," Sister Toni instructed. Then she put her arm around Jesse's narrow shoulders and led her from the room full of children, all tossing and adjusting and calling goodnight.

Jesse stood outside of the door, comfy in the fold of Sister Toni's habit, her side warm against Toni's lean hardness, the cold mountain air settling and swirling around them.

"You have a gift with the children." Sister Toni spoke, standing still, watching the deepening night.

"They make me feel safe when I put them to bed," Jesse replied, holding tightly and not moving.

"Do you believe in the story you told?"

"It's just a story my mother told me."

"But do you believe in the healing waters?" Sister Toni persisted.

"That's magic, Sister, I thought the church doesn't believe in magic."

"Even the church doesn't understand all the ways that God works." Sister Toni was quiet for a moment, reflecting on her own words. "I watched your face and I could see the longing in your eyes, so I am asking you again, do you believe in your mother's story?

"I want to."

"And what do you want the water to heal?"

Jesse was silent for a while then answered.

"I don't know, Sister. When I'm alone it's like I'm not really there, like I'm just watching this girl who is all by herself. It scares me. I'm afraid of what I might do, of what might happen. Sister, I want my Mom to come make it okay, to take away these feelings, but she can't; she's not here, not anymore."

"And your father?"

"I have no father. I had a foster-father once. He's gone. I'm glad he's gone."

Together they stood again in silence, Sister Toni's arm still around Jesse's fragile shoulders. Sister Toni thought about their words, and Jesse's story and the mountains she loved and about hope. The kind of hope that makes things better, that makes bad times bearable. As she had these thoughts, she looked out toward the one mountain that towered above the others, dark and foreboding and framed by the stars. She wondered about Jesse's story, about the similarity of the name of Jesse's mountain to the mountain before her, the Rock Candy Mountain. She contemplated the mysteries of God and the difficulty in understanding His will. She had always been torn between the comforting assumption that God, if asked, would direct every aspect of her life and her suspicion that for the most part, she was on her own. On occasion, she would feel moved to act but she was never sure if that prompting came from God or from herself. On those particular occasions though, she knew in her heart that the promptings were right, that one way or another it was the course of conduct that she should follow.

Sister Toni stood in the cold and the chill and thought about Jesse who was huddled close and she felt that familiar certainty. It was time to act, time to help this young girl. She turned to Jesse, her hands now on each of Jesse's shoulders.

"Jesse, I don't think God can help us if we just sit around and worry things to death. I think we need to act, to address this sadness of yours head on. I think that we should go on an adventure. We're standing here in the foothills of the Rock Candy Mountain. It's had that name for as long as I can remember. I think it just might be the same mountain as the one in your story. You and I are going to climb that mountain and find the living water and fill your empty spaces and put a smile back on your face."

More certain than ever of the rightness of her plan, she looked carefully at Jesse. She saw no reaction.

"That's just an old story, Sister."

"Well, it may just be an old story but it's our story now," Sister Toni said firmly. "We'll leave in the morning," she added, almost to herself, as she pushed Jesse towards the bunkhouse.

"Sleep child," Sister Toni ordered, then turned and walked slowly towards her hut. As she walked, she looked up and saw a dark wall of clouds filling the sky to the north. The clouds were moving deliberately towards her, turning off the stars one by one.

Jesse was not sure what to think. She wondered if Sister Toni was actually going to take her off into the wilderness. For a moment, she felt both a small prod of excitement and a quiver of fear as she looked out at the dark shapes in the distance. Hugging herself for a moment, she watched Toni's back slipping away into the dark night then she turned and entered the bunkhouse.

Before entering her own hut, Sister Toni sat on the wooden bench that a local mountain man had built for her at the beginning of the summer. She smiled to herself as she remembered his brief visit. He had dug postholes and swept the cabins and built and cursed and filled the whole settlement with his exuberance. He was inordinately proud of his abstinence from alcohol for three entire days. She could still hear his words as she sat before him on this same rough-hewn bench. "Goddamn, 'scuse me Sister, (he was always cursing and always apologizing) but I feel like a million bucks, the air is so clean and sweet (and he'd demonstrate by drawing in a lungful) and I can feel the breezes rushing over the hairs on my arms, can you figger that?" He exclaimed, holding out his hand and arm and turning it back and forth in wonder. "Goddamn—sorry Sister—but I am a new man, I'm telling you, a new man," and he would look up at her and smile with his wide tooth-gapping smile. He was truly engaging, that man.

But four days proved too much apparently, for that very night, without a word, he packed his old clothes, the ones she had washed and folded herself, and was gone. He left a bit of a hole, an empty spot.

Sister Toni sighed, thinking again about the here-and-now as she rested in the work wrought by Mac's hand, her just-found certainty already beginning to crumble. Now what have I done? I am definitely getting too old for this kind of foolishness, climbing a mountain, my God. And what if nothing is there? There's no good reason that anything will be there. Am I setting the poor child up for another disappointment? What possessed me in the first place? Sister Toni sat and listened for a while, letting her mind slowly loosen and be open to the sounds of the night, the soft rattling of the tamaracks in the wind, the deep hoot of a pair of owls calling to each other, echoing back and forth, and the sound of water falling somewhere in the distance. She listened to the soft full sounds of silence and soon found that an answer to her own worries and questions, as it often did, became clear.

She slowly got up and stretched her knees and joints and with hands again tender from the cold, opened the door to her hut and entered to sleep. She and Jesse would need an early start.

Toni fell asleep thinking of Mac.

CHAPTER THREE

Over hill over dale
Through bush, through brier
Over park over pale
Through flood through fire
I do wander ever where. ₃

Mac woke, reeking from the stink of sweat and tequila. When he tried to claw his way out of his gunnysack his arms stuck in the narrow opening. He panicked and for a moment found he couldn't push his arms up or out then finally freed one arm and struggled to sit up. Breathing harshly into the darkness he pushed his other arm above his head, grabbed the bag with both hands, then pushed it down past his shoulders. "God damn it!" He exploded, "God damn it!" he repeated, then rose to his knees and immediately lost his balance and fell over on his side. Prone, he pushed the bag over his legs and crawled out of its grasp, kicking it off of his feet. He crawled up on his hands and knees, shaking, carefully perched on all fours.

Covered with sweat, Mac rocked back and forth. His hands and knees were chilled by the frost covered ground. His pounding heart gradually slowed as the sweat began to cool on his old frame and the cold started to burn. He finally struggled to his feet, his head down, his cold hands rubbing his cold knees. "God damn it!" Mac exclaimed once more, now less a yell, more a heavy sigh, as he slowly stood upright, his back creaking, for the first time aware of the dark woods that surrounded him.

In front of Mac the night pressed closely. He peered into its midst but couldn't determine its depth or density. Behind him and to his left Mac heard water running, rushing and falling over rocks, and he was suddenly seized by an overpowering thirst. He slowly edged towards the sound of the water, still unable to see the ground. He stood unmoving for a moment and just as he was about to take a step, he heard a twig crack off to his right. Mac looked towards the sound, listening, holding his breath, but heard only silence and the rushing of his own blood. He slowly let his breath out then heard what sounded like two footfalls, one quickly following the other, and then it was silent again. His heart began again to accelerate with his fear, pain pulsing now behind his eyes and forehead. He hurriedly slapped his pockets searching for his pistol or a knife then bent down and felt the bone handle of the slender knife he kept strapped to his left calf.

Mac slowly pulled the blade and straightened up, cocking his head, still hearing nothing, aware only of the call of the water and the rhythm of his forehead pounding in time with his beating heart. He stood quietly in the forest, wondering how he had managed to wake up hung-over in the middle of no-where. Wondering if his nightmare of sticking a gun in some guy's face and Lucky's head blowing up was real or part of his tequila-fevered imagination. His gut churned and a familiar black despair began to sweep over him, hastened by the uncertainty in his own mind and the image of blood spewing from Lucky's head as he toppled backwards.

The silence grew, broken only by the persistent call of the falling water. Mac licked his dry lips. He wasn't sure how long he stood, holding his knife and waiting, but eventually he realized that the trees had definition and he could begin to see the lay of the ground. He was carefully stepping over a flat rock when a mule deer exploded out of the darkness. Mac jumped away, almost falling, then grabbing at the rough bark of a tree with his bare hand as the deer bounded right then left up the hill.

"Judas Priest!" Mac swore softly, then cautiously stepped over roots and rocks, and around trees until he reached a black pool fed by the rushing stream. He knelt down and buried his head in the cold dark water, then raised his head and drank deeply. He gasped once before bending to drink again, the water so cold that his throat and forehead ached.

Mac sat back on the wet tree roots, watching the woods surrounding him slowly appear, sitting back and worrying about Lucky, remembering last night's events as if they were rolling out of a dense fog, a fog that cleared as the rising sun filtered out the dark and the shadows from the forest, remembering with shame his panic and yellow fear.

Mac had turned after the gunshots and lifted Lucky in his arms. He had a vivid memory of running from the roadway and then falling forward over the edge of a cliff. Little by little, he remembered struggling to crawl down the rocks and fissures. He recalled reaching out into the darkness and feeling for the stranger's body, for Lucky, calling in a panicked whisper to the darkness and getting no response, afraid to call out loud. When he reached a flat area at the bottom of the ravine, he had stopped, sobbing, hurting all over, waiting for a bullet to come from the darkness and strike him. Finally, he had slipped off his pack and pulled out a battered metal flask from the inside of his coat pocket. Raising the cold metal to his lips, he had sucked down the burning liquid, killing the fear and the pain and shivering with cold, then drinking, again and again.

◆ ◆ ◆ ◆

Late that same night, Moses McLaren leaned back in his oversized pine rocker, his worn boots resting lightly on the planked floor. His rifle, still scented with the spent sulfur of shots fired, lay heavy against his thin legs. The room was dark except for the darting light and dancing shadows thrown from the fire. He sat without moving, hands resting on the now cold metal of the gun, listening to the wind as it howled outside of the window, staring at nothing.

It was no good. His jumbled attempt to set things straight put nothing behind him. From the time McLaren had borne witness to his son's violent death he had spent his evenings pacing back and forth the length of his house, waiting for sleep, needing to move, tormented by his failure to act. He would walk until his legs wouldn't hold him any longer and then he would fall asleep in his chair and the nightmares would begin. He was tormented by images of both his son, who had been hunted down and Anna, whose death he'd struggled for years to forget. He was unable to separate one from the other.

In his troubled mind he had convinced himself that he could only justify his daughter's passing by avenging his son and he had failed.

So he sat and slowly rocked back and forth, the planks creaking beneath him, cedar planks that he had crafted as a young man. Those had been simpler times, easier times. He remembered when he and his Pa had felled the trees and struggled with the jump saw that cut each length. He could still smell the sweet weeping of the cut timbers, could feel the stick of the pitch and dark black dirt that had covered his hands at the end of the day. While his Pa watched he would carefully stack the cut wood flat on the rocks, letting it cure, slowly creating his future home piece by piece.

Back then his world had been a big place. He'd wake in the early morning and hike up the nearest ridgeline and look out over the sea of trees and cascading waves of mountains and know that he was part of all that he could see. He remembered wild times in those forests, winter nights when he and others would circle a massive fire fueled by the jettison of their logging, the fire's flames reaching so high into the trees that the heat from the fire would explode pockets of ice and snow into puffs of steam and water that fell on the men below, fell on their laughter and awkward dance around the swoosh and crackle of the flames.

Then a son was born. From the time the boy could walk, he would place his small hand within Moses's and they would forage into the dense forests and hidden crevices searching for treasure. Some mornings they would rise before dawn and lay silently in the grasses waiting for the deer to cautiously leave their bedding grounds and move towards the valley springs to drink. Moses's world grew to include all the places he hoped to share with his son, all the new places they would explore.

And then somewhere along the way Ian sheered off course. He began to spend more and more time alone. Though they had never talked much, Moses found his entreaties quietly ignored, his rough touch often avoided. His first-born was slowly changing into something that he didn't recognize, didn't want to recognize, and Moses did not know what to do. Finally there came a time when he quit looking too closely, closed his ears to the gossip he'd hear, the stories that folks would tell. It was then that his world quit growing.

When Moses lost his wife his perspective darkened and his world began to shrink. He was afraid of seeing his world the way it had been with her at his side, afraid to come to grips with her absence. He began to limit his world to the here and now, concrete tasks that required his immediate attention, but nothing more. He began to spend more time staring into the amber bottom of his cup than embracing the vast wild spaces that surrounded him. Then Anna was gone and things got smaller yet, and now Ian *was* dead.

Moses was in a hole, deep and fearful with no way out. The constant companion to the haunting image of his son's naked corpse was the picture of Anna's small frail body awkwardly resting on that soiled hospital bed. He had found her lying there, her form lit by the fractured sheen of the streetlight that pierced the room's single window. Her hands had been twisted into her bedclothes as if she were trying to hold on, hold back what was coming. Her emaciated arms and legs were covered with purple and yellowed bruises.

Moses sat in his rocker, plagued by that particular memory. He had been perched on a broken plastic chair in the darkened room, leaning forward, long arms on boney knees, shoulders silently shaking at the sight of his pitiful, lifeless little girl. The little girl who he'd turned his back on, who he hadn't seen since their last fight when he'd reached out and slapped her, full of frustration and shame and righteous anger.

"God damn you Anna!" he had cried. "How dare you shame this house, shame me!" And she just stared at him, her eyes hardening with hate and filling with tears and then she turned and ran out the door and he stood there and did nothing but close the door and pour a drink.

Moses had gotten the word from the new sheriff. They didn't know one another. The sheriff had stood at his threshold, his hat in hand, both feet shuffling, his eyes looking anywhere but at Moses. They'd found his daughter and it wasn't pretty. Moses rushed to the hospital and stood in that room across from his daughter's battered form, surrounded by his shame and the rising and falling rumble of the cars and trucks climbing the grade next to the old brick hospital. Overcome by it all he collapsed into that cheap hospital chair and slowly filled with loathing for himself and after a time for all the others, just on the other side of the dirt-stained window, others who were consumed with their piss-ant little problems and cared nothing for his little girl. He dealt with his grief the only way he knew how, with anger, brooding and full of hate. An anger that thrust itself outward, encompassing all of the self-important pricks and assholes who rushed to get one meaningless thing done so they could do another meaningless thing, not knowing or caring that his daughter lay broken and lifeless before him.

Moses was also haunted by memories whose torment surpassed even the evocations of guilt over Anna's death. These were the memories of the good times, the joy that he could touch no longer. There was a time long ago when Anna would sit cross legged in front of the stone fireplace he'd built with his own hands, playing with a handful of tamarack knots, polished to a shiny gray. Her "ol' bones," he had called them, as they would knock softly together in her hands. He remembered her laughing as they would drop from her grasp, looking up at him, confident that he shared her amusement, and then she would lean against his leg, humming in the firelight. "Tell me a story Daddy," she would say, "Tell me a story." And he would lean back, his massive hand resting on her head and with his other hand lift the cup of whiskey to his lips and sip a little and start to talk. He could remember being full of life at those times, full of her contentment.

Lately he'd been having a recurrent dream. He'd dream that Anna had opened her eyes that night in the hospital. In his dream, sitting right next to her, with her hand on the child's forehead, was Anna's mother who had died birthing her. And his little girl spoke to him. She said, "It's alright, I'm okay now," over and over and then she would reach out and touch Moses's hand and he would feel, just for an instant, that it might be okay, that the hole in his chest could fill a little and he wouldn't hurt so bad. Later he'd wake, but he'd never permit himself to feel okay; he knew he had no right, no right at all.

Now he sat with his hands on his rifle, his elbows on the arms of the rocker with his head tipped back. He kept thinking about his little girl. He had talked to her at the hospital, while she was lying there in front of him. He told her he was sorry he'd struck her, sorry he'd not come running from the house begging her forgiveness and asking her to stay home, stay with him, but there was no response. The dead don't talk.

◆ ◆ ◆ ◆

When daylight fully broke Mac finally shook off the haze and bleakness of the tequila. He found himself consumed by a sense of urgency. His skin was clammy and damp. He was suddenly restless, uneasy in his present state.

What was he doin' sitting here? He had to find that stranger and Lucky. Christ, they may both be alive and dying as he sat there on his skinny ass trembling from the tequila jitters. He struggled up and scanned the cliffs, now clearly etched in the morning sun. He knew he was somewhere in the Hell Creek gorge but wasn't sure where they had gone over the side. He picked out an old black pine that split about ten feet off the ground, both sides growing horizontally for a few feet and then twisting and turning upward again, and marked it in his mind. Setting off he followed the base of the cliff upstream from the tree, watching for any sign of anything. He walked for ten minutes, seeing only a few deer at the water's edge and the shadow of something larger moving across the creek.

Mac stopped. Something to his right had caught his eye. He looked closely and could just make out a faint trail leading down from the cliffs. The trail crossed in front of him, heading towards the water, then turned upstream. Bending down he reached for a bit of branch that was broken and pushed into the mud of the trail. Tracing it lightly with his forefinger, he studied the path ahead, eyes tracking a small piece of the trail at a time.

Abruptly he stood and stacked three flat rocks on top of a larger stone, then turned and worked his way back to the twisted tree, this time traveling closer to the creek, scrambling over boulders and stacked piles of limbs resting precariously against one another in the drainage. Old rocks and old trees whitened with age.

As he was crawling over one of the fallen limbs, he saw the stranger. He was lying near the creek, one side of his face flat against a smooth slab of gray-black stone. Mac could see a rusted smear of blood on the stranger's forehead, contrasting starkly with his white skin and pale gray hair.

When Buck opened his eyes he saw Mac's old grizzled face staring down at him, smiling.

"Well, good," Mac said, "You woke up. I thought maybe you were a goner."

Mac squatted down beside Buck. "Lay still, I need to check ye' for injuries."

He touched Buck's boots, turning them slightly, then slowly moved his hands upward touching and pressing each limb and joint in turn, ending with Buck's head. His touch was gentle. Buck lay tense but still, hurting, but not at Mac's touch. To Buck, things were all out of kilter, as if he wasn't quite there lying on a rock in a deep gorge with this weird old guy touching him. He didn't feel any compulsion to move away until Mac touched his forehead. Then Buck jerked away from the touch, pain shooting from his forehead, and Mac pulled away, lifting his hands.

"Okay, okay, now don't be a candy-ass, you're not hurt that bad." Mac leaned over, carefully putting his arm behind Buck's back and helping him to sit up. He offered him his canteen before sitting back on his heels to watch Buck drink.

"So boyo are we havin' fun yet?" Mac's bushy eyebrows rose up in question. Buck closed his eyes for a minute, feeling a dull ache from the front of his head, then slowly opened his eyes again, taking in the granite of the cliffs and the sound of the water rushing past just below.

"Who the hell are you?" He asked.

Mac watched Buck, his eyes distant for a moment and then said, "Well, as to who I am, I guess it depends on your perspective now doesn't it?" Uninvited, Mac scooted to a spot on the rock just next to Buck. He sat there, adjusting a little, then turned towards Buck.

"Most would call me Mac, and you?"

"Buck. Call me Buck."

"You took a bit of a fall. It 'pears that you were lucky enough to land on a tree," Mac said pointing, "Instead of this here rock." Mac slowly reached over and took the canteen out of Buck's hand, lifting it to his own mouth, and took two or three long swallows.

"Sorry about last night. I guess I drank a little too much tequila and felt like Robin Hood." He grinned. "It's hell getting old." He put the lid back on the canteen and handed it back to Buck.

"Now you sit here for a stretch and don't be movin' around too much. I need to check out a few things." Mac stood and stretched a bit then jumped over to another granite slab and off onto the ground, disappearing into the trees and tall ferns that lined the falling creek. By the time Buck could croak, "Wait!" Mac was long gone and Buck slowly leaned back and closed his eyes.

Buck woke again when he heard Mac's whistling approach. His head was feeling better. He reached for the pine next to him and pulled himself up. Mac appeared with two packs in hand. He set the packs down, walked up to Buck, pulled some jerky out of a bag he had hung around his neck and offered it.

"Eat."

Buck took a slice of jerky and broke a piece off with his teeth. He washed the jerky down with a sip from the canteen and then drank again, the water still cold. He handed the canteen back to Mac.

"What happened to the red headed kid?" remembering the spray of blood.

"Well, he must be okay," Mac responded, talking while he chewed on a piece of jerky. "He's not on the road, and it looks like he took off up the gorge trail with that mule of yours; saw some sign up-creek, not a lot of blood. Found the rest of Lucky's and my gear though, right near the cliff where we fell." He gestured toward the two loaded pack frames, sitting next to the trail, near the creek. "I guess Lucky's got your stuff."

Buck asked, "Who shot him?"

Mac rubbed his face with both hands before he answered. "Well, I suspect it was McLaren. The kid got into it with the old man's boy. From what I heard it wasn't pretty. Lucky, he's got a little temper problem, don't like people being hurt."

"Who got hurt?" Buck asked, and then continued, "How bad did Lucky beat him up?"

Mac stopped tearing off jerky and looked at Buck. "Don't matter now. What's done's done." He broke eye contact and looked away. "Didn't beat him up though, he killed 'im."

Mac then bent and slung one pack on his back and grabbed the other in his hand and headed up the creek. He yelled back over his shoulder, "I'd stay close," before he disappeared into the trees.

Buck hesitated for a minute. He glanced apprehensively up at the gray cliffs surrounding him. Feeling more alone every second, he hurried to follow. Pushing aside the branches of a blue fir, he could see a faint trail stretching ahead of him. He was thinking that things definitely weren't okay, thinking that his wife was not going to believe this shit. As he hurried down the path, ducking under the low hanging limbs and jumping from one stone to another, he was suddenly struck with the realization that he was enjoying himself. His head was pounding, he could taste the morning in the fragrant damp air, the sunlight was bounding off the brilliant green leaves and blue gray water, warming his face and arms, and he was running after this weird old guy with a homicidal friend. "Jesus," he muttered as he jumped to yet another chunk of granite, "I'm fucking losing it."

CHAPTER FOUR

What hempen homespuns have we
swaggering here
So near the cradle of the Fairy Queen? 4

The sun was warm and high by the time Mac and Buck crawled out of the canyon. As Buck pulled himself over the last outcrop of rock and yellow moss, he was stunned by the enormity of a mountain that filled the space before him. Massive formations of green blue stone pushed upwards, high above the tree choked ravines and alpine ridges. Buck had to tip his head back to see what appeared to be the summit.

"Look at that," Buck exclaimed, "Look at that!" gesturing to Mac, "It's incredible."

"It's a lot bigger and further than it looks," Mac responded.

"That's it isn't it? The Rock Candy Mountain, son of a bitch." Buck stood and stared, tasting the scent of cold stone and thin air.

"You know, that's why I made this trip, to see that mountain." Buck gently shook his head, touching his forehead where it had been pounding earlier that morning. Turning to his left, he could see the uneven line of the canyon cutting its way to the north and west, the last of it narrowing to a thin dark line. To the east, the hills rolled away in sharp waves, each successive ridgeline a lighter shade of blue and purple than the one before it. Purple mountain majesty, just like the damn song, he thought.

Sore and tired, he settled on the sloping moss-covered rock beside him. He listened to the soft murmur of water from the gorge below then heard a quick but fleeting hum from the forest to his right.

He looked at Mac who gestured with his lips to a stand of aspens, their leaves spinning, brilliant yellow against the blue sky and gray granite. "Aspen leaves, sound like that in the wind."

After a moment he continued. "Sometimes the tamaracks, when it's real cold and blowing, start to dance, swinging back and forth, their tops heavy with snow and ice. When they twist and bend they make a sound just like a fuckin' orchestra of fairy flutes coming right out of the hillside. Scared me good more'n once." Mac stood up. He was more animated than

Buck had seen him since he had been brandishing his rifle the night before. He pointed to the exposed rock on a ridge leading up to the mountain, "You see that greenish blue rock? It's called bluestone, magic rock. Folks say the only place you can find it is right here on this mountain." Mac stopped. He looked at Buck sheepishly, embarrassed by his show of enthusiasm.

"What's it good for?" Buck asked, "I mean the rock?"

"Hell, I don't know," Mac answered, the shine that had lit his eyes when he talked of the tamaracks and bluestone leaving as quickly as it had appeared. "The tree rats crawl around here in the summer filling their rusted-out pile of shit pick-ups with it, so I guess somebody's buying."

"Tree rats?"

Mac sat down on the moss-covered slab they just had crawled around, wiping his face with one sleeve of his coat, a face full of color and sweat. His eyes focusing after a time back in Buck's direction.

There's a lot you don't know about these parts," Mac said, grimacing as he worked something out between his teeth with his forefinger.

"What the hell are tree rats?" Buck asked again.

Mac just looked at him, fingering his tooth.

"I 'spect you're a city boy, nice clothes and all." He raised his eyebrows, questioning.

"Close enough," Buck answered.

Mac nodded, "Figured."

He worked at his teeth for a while then turned away, cleared his throat, and spat into the dirt. Looking back at Buck, he asked, "So boyo, where do you want to go from here?

"I'm not sure," Buck responded.

"Do you know where my truck is?"

Mac looked back over the gorge and pointed to a point to the southeast. "See that patch of yellow? Just above that is where the road crosses the gorge. The truck was, was," he emphasized, "Around there."

"What do you mean was?"

"Well, while you were snoozing back in the gorge I ran on up to the top to check for Lucky, to make sure he got out of there, you know. And anyways, he was gone and so was your rig. I suppose that McLaren or whoever was shootin' probably took it." Mac smiled at Buck and gave a little shrug.

"So what's next Bucko?"

Buck sat for a minute and wasn't quite sure how to answer. He didn't care much about the truck, but he found he was unnerved by the loss of the shotgun. The double barrel LC Smith had been in his family for generations. His grandpa had bragged about its accuracy, though Buck had no recollection of him shooting it. It probably hadn't been used to hunt for fifty years. Buck had only shot it a few weeks ago in the field behind the house. It was just an heirloom, he figured, but for some reason he couldn't dismiss its loss that easily. It meant something. It was a connection to older times, to parts of him long hidden away.

Damn. He was suddenly weary of all of this. His truck was stolen, the shotgun gone, and he was sitting on this fucking rock in the middle of nowhere, sore and tired.

Looking over at Mac he finally responded, "Hell, I don't know."

He took a few more deep breaths, forcing his thoughts to the present. "You think we can find my donkey?"

Yeah," Mac responded, nodding his head. "I 'spect we can do that."

Buck sat on the rock, his butt cold, the mountain massive before him, filling his perspective. He was feeling again that he had no way to place himself in all this, no starting point. He felt the warm sun on his face and the comfy ache of his muscles, heated and stretched from the climb. He took another deep breath, and the scent of cedar and cold ice and clean air rushed through him, pulled at him. It both scared and attracted him, all at the same time. There was something new out here he could gain sustenance from, something far different from his tightly constructed memories and fragile past. As he considered this he felt a familiar flutter of apprehension in his gut, a small touch of fear and foreboding that he pushed away, looking beyond it, letting the place and circumstances fill his senses. He stood up, stretching muscles tightened by the brief rest and looked at Mac, right into his crazy bloodshot eyes.

"Let's go get my goddamn donkey." Buck said, finding himself smiling at his own tough words. He added, "I don't even know why I'm smiling at you, you old bastard, but here we are."

"Yeah, well, I kinda have that effect on folks," Mac responded, smiling in return.

Then Mac pulled his flask from his side pocket and took a swallow, capped it and stood up. "Hope you're up to it boyo." He looked at Buck appraisingly then tossed the spare pack at Buck's feet and walked past him, following a narrow twisting trail along the ledge. He called out, "I think Lucky and that mule of yours went that-a-ways," and he pointed with his right hand directly at the mountain.

Buck and Mac hiked for an hour, mostly in silence, concentrating as their packs got heavier and pulled at the muscles in their necks and shoulders, following the edge of the gorge and winding slowly up towards the steeper slopes of the mountain. When the trail turned from the gorge and appeared to head directly into the trees, Mac stopped and leaned back against the hill.

"Break time."

Buck sat down beside him, winded, slowly rubbing his thighs with his hands. Turning to Mac, he asked, "So are you going to tell me what a tree rat is?"

Mac took a quick sip from his flask, shook it, then dug in his pack for a bottle. After he carefully topped off the flask and packed away the bottle, he started to talk.

"Well, I guess you could say I'm a tree rat," he said. "You know the world you come from with all of its long sufferin', rigid, uptight types, well, that world doesn't have a place for some folks. You may not see it, but you follow a pretty narrow path with your codes and fancy churches and superstores full of junk and your skinny white toothed, uptight, tight assed prom-queen wives. We're the guys who make you nervous when we sit next to you in the restaurant, that carry guns in our rigs and get puking drunk at your weddings. We live out here." He waved generally around him and nodded, affirming himself. "Course, a damn tree rat shot Lucky, so you see we don't always get along neither."

After a time Mac pocketed the flask and said, "Well, let's go on a bit more; I know a spot to camp." And with that Mac heaved himself up, and turning away from the gorge, entered the forest. Buck was right behind him.

Later that evening the sun was setting on Buck's second night in the mountains. To his left, a small fire, gold and blue, reflected against the black rocks and the skeletal shadows of the forest. Mac squatted near the fire, his lined and haggard face lit up by the dance of the flames.

Sitting back, leaning against a rock, the air now cold with the evening's chill, Buck thought of the strangeness of his circumstances. Aside from Mac's silent presence across the fire, he was alone, and if he had to rely on his own devices, lost. His companion was likely crazy, a drunk, and twenty-four hours ago was robbing him. It was a world apart from what he was used to. The last normal human being he had talked to was his wife, who stood on their porch and warned him about grizzlies. He wondered what she would think about Mac.

That morning, the morning before he had left, he and his wife had been sitting near the edge of the pond that skirted the west side of their home. The pond was filled with dark blue water and littered with curling and yellowed lily pads. He sat on a boulder they had hired a kid to place. The rock was damp and cool and the rising sun warm on his face. He watched his wife move along the shoreline, picking up twigs that had fallen from the trees and cutting back flowers that she had planted along the edge of the water.

"I wonder when the first frost will hit," Buck asked.

She looked up and shrugged, poking at the dirt, then said, "I think the flowers are about gone," and continued cutting and lifting leaves and peering at the blossom buds left to open.

"Here, use my shirt." Buck pulled off his t-shirt, his skin rising with goose bumps, and handed it to her to hold the flowers now overflowing in her long and narrow hands. Buck closed his eyes and after a moment passed he felt her touch, warm and light, slowly kneading his shoulders, then moving down his back. He could feel her hair tickling his skin and smell her scent as she leaned over him.

"Hey there," she said, and Buck stirred with the soft morning and dew-scented woman standing next to him, her hands tracing a pattern on his back, then under his arms, just below his ribs. For a moment, he absently touched her hands, tracing her fingers with his, but he found himself uncomfortable with the intimacy. Suddenly restless, anxious to move, he lifted his hands away and stood up. "I'll get us some coffee."

Buck walked across the yard to the house. By the time he had poured both cups, she had come in after him, setting the flowers in the sink and tossing his t-shirt back to him. After handing his wife her mug, he took a sip of his own and set it down on the counter.

"Well, I'd better get packed up."

He glanced over at her as he spoke the words unsuccessfully trying to catch her eye, then walked out to the barn to get the donkey.

Loading his gear, he had wondered what she was thinking. He wondered whether that bit of hurt and question in her eyes meant that she assumed he had found their home or her wanting, or maybe she just thought he was goofy as hell. He wondered why he was going anywhere.

Now, Buck sat by the fire in the growing dark and thought about her and about being without her. His memories of her touch were enflamed by the rawness of his immediate experience and last night's muse of their younger days. Son of a bitch, he thought, I shouldn't have left that way, just walking off. He recognized his lack of attention that morning, his preoccupation with this damn trip, seeing, now, how it must have appeared to her. His sense of isolation grew as he began to see the distance between them for what it was. He saw how she pulled back, afraid or confused by the promptings that drove him. He understood that he was most at ease when there was just a little distance between him and others. He sat, cold and tired in the dirt, watching the approaching night and was slowly overwhelmed by his loneliness. The panic and fear that he'd, until now, successfully kept at bay, returned, crushing him with a sense of dread that tightened his chest until it seemed that he could no longer bear it.

Abruptly, by an act of will, he forced himself to ignore the hopelessness that threatened to engulf him. Struggling to his feet he focused on the fire and the night, on slowing down, centering himself in the present, breathing in and tasting the scent of burning wood, aware of the formidable presence of the mountain hidden in the dark.

He quietly called out, "Hey Mac."

Mac looked up at Buck and asked, "You ever been shot boyo?"

Buck looked at Mac as he sat in the shadows behind the fire.

"No, Jesus! Why would you ask me that?"

"Why not? I was thinkin' about Lucky and about tree rats and about you. Mostly about you. You know I 'spect in your world nothing really ever happens, other than dying, which we all do. What do you worry most about anyways? Paying your bills?"

Mac shifted as he talked, leaning forward towards the fire, firelight flickering across his face.

"Probably those stupid-ass bills I'm guessing, or maybe it's screwin' your secretary, if you're man enough, or manicuring your little patch of green. I can surely see that picture, you runnin' around in your shorts and wife-beater, squirting poison on plants that don't meet your goddamn definition of what fits. Fancy house, phony jerk-offs, you have no idea how quickly all that could be gone, how quickly all that could count for nothin'." Mac's eyes were hard and bright now in the flames. "One little bitty piece of lead could shatter your bones and rip your muscles and splatter your thin skittery blood, dead as dead before your piss and water soak into the ground."

Then Mac was silent, his words replaced by the sound of wind in the trees and the rattle of rocks falling nearby.

Mac suddenly jumped up, crossed over to Buck and bent down, sticking his face and stinking breath right up next to Buck's. Buck pulled back in alarm.

"But you never know, bucko," Mac growled, his raspy voice edged with anger. "I may not know anything. Maybe I'm just an envious old bastard that can't hold a job, one of those fucking losers in your book." Mac stood back up. For a moment, his eyes, wild and bright, were focused intently on Buck's face, then the craziness began to fade, Mac's rigid features softened and he turned and sat heavily on the dirt and grass next to Buck. He was quiet for a minute, subdued, his words spent. He slowly shook his head and then continued.

"Don't matter. Out here none of it matters at all."

Mac reached into the folds of his worn and torn jacket and pulled out his flask.

"So here's to you boyo."

He upended it, eyes closed. Lowering it, he breathed hoarsely, "Goddamn, that hits the spot," and thrust the flask in Buck's direction.

"Knock one down; it'll put hair on your chest."

Hesitating for a moment, Buck shook his head then reached out and grabbed the flask, wet with Mac's sweat and grease, and tossed it back, the tequila slowly worked its way down his throat, burning his gut, washing his thoughts clean, leaving a sense of calm, of well-being, of two beings well met.

"Goddamn."

Buck took another sip.

"Goddamn, you are one weird fucker, Mac."

Mac and Buck both sat then, their backs against the fallen log, sharing sips and watching the broad lit sky, crisscrossed with streaking stars and milky ways. As they drank, they both pushed back the boogey-man that stood as a shared specter before them. Past's specter of failure and failed courage. They shared stories part true and part made up of drink and the strangeness of their company, and talked about kids and home and lonely times.

Mac began to talk about his wanders. He talked of when he'd head out in the spring and be gone for weeks following the haunting call of the geese overhead. He was always heading north, pushing further and further into the wilderness. Each spring he'd follow this call but always came dragging back, leaving a bit of himself behind, till finally one year he didn't come back at all. He stayed out here but found that he was still losing himself, a little at a time, sometimes by forgetting, sometimes losing himself in the flask that always inhabited his coat pocket. He'd search for all those lost parts but there was never anything to find.

Mac leaned back against the log, looking up into the thick blanket of stars, and told Buck how he'd spend time at night trying to remember what the girl he had fallen for, a long time ago, looked like. She was strong. He remembered that. She'd hold his head in her hands and look him in the eye and then smile and tell him that he was a fuckin' train wreck. He remembered that too. Sometimes she would hold him with her thighs wrapped around him and her arms pulling him close, and those times he never wanted to be anywhere but right there with her. And she'd laugh, mostly at him. He had liked it when she laughed. But her face wasn't so clear anymore, no matter how hard he tried to picture her. "She's out there in the distance," Mac explained, looking at

Buck and pointing to the dark shadows of the valley below them. "Out there and moving slowly away, you understand me, Bucko, un'erstand how it is?" And Buck nodded in the dark, "Yeah Mac, I'm with you, I understand."

Buck's lips were numb with the booze but his imagination was alive. The tequila-tinted raw emotions were rushing through him and Mac's pain and loneliness was shared and heartfelt.

"I'm with you Mac."

And as time passed they began to laugh together and howl at the stars, and eventually Buck fell asleep, dreaming that he was falling through the air, patiently waiting to hit the ground.

◆ ◆ ◆ ◆

Some time after Mac and Buck had curled up near the dying fire and slept their restless tequila sleep, the sun was rising over a valley on another side of the mountain. Sister Toni gently shook Jesse's shoulder. "Wake up now little one, we must be underway before the sun gets too high." Jesse turned and stared blankly for a moment at Sister Toni and then her eyes filled with understanding. She crawled out of her bedding and into the cold, dressed and hurried out of the bunkhouse, one pack over her shoulder and another in her hand.

Sister Toni greeted her.

"Let's go climb a mountain."

Her voice was first tempered with a small smile, then a bigger smile as she soaked in the beauty of the morning and clean air and Jesse's grin, all so full of God's hope.

◆ ◆ ◆ ◆

Later in the morning, the cold also greeted Buck and Mac as they crawled out of their bags, the tequila churning their stomachs. They fumbled with twigs and moss and started a fire. Once the fire was throwing off heat and the coffee was perking, they both sat back, wrapped in a shared post-drunk fog. That state of being where your nerves are raw and emotions are too close to the surface. Buck smiled grimly, reminded painfully of why he usually avoided chugging tequila and looked over his cup at Mac.

"Why do you stay in the mountains Mac?"

Mac grunted, "I don't know, too lazy to go anywhere else I guess." He sat up, stretching his back, working out the kinks. "The thing is, Bucko, there's nothing in your world for me, nothin' real. These hills and rocks and cold winters and this hangover. That's real enough for me." Mac paused, then pushed himself back against a felled tree and pulled out his stained flask. He gave it a good look before carefully putting it back in his pocket.

"I once had a life outside of here, outside of this valley."

Mac stared out over the drainage that lay below them, the sun rising over the top of the ridge, touching the tops of the trees to the west. He stared as if he could see something other than the trees and rocks and early morning mist. After a time he rubbed his worn face with his trembling hands, then scooting himself up a little, leaned back against the smooth wood. He looked over at Buck and wondered where to start. He had been a brash young man, he remembered that, a young buck full of himself, full to the brim. He had plans, big plans cooking about in his head. He was always thinking. Sometimes his head worked so fast he had a hard time keeping up with it. Sometimes he was just so full of gumption that he would find himself on a heart-thumpin' tear, jumping off a moving freight train or slamming his fist into John Hardy's fat face or pressing himself into the firm muscled length of a woman's flanks, losing himself and shouting and swingin' then suddenly realizing that it was all gone, the big empty bad feeling washing over him like a cold rain, missed train, hard slam of hard ground, John's tearing eyes, asking "What the hell, Mac," and a crying white tangle of legs and hands and smeared mascara watching him as he stared at his own tired face in a rusted mirror.

"I always seemed to be getting into one fix or another. Trying to make things right, trying to get away. I did a lot of that, gettin' away," Mac said staring at the backs of his rough-veined hands.

"I walked away from the young girls I'd been with, and asshole bosses and school and stupid teachers and la di la swells." Mac looked up at Buck, his eyes alive now in the telling. "But it was never terminal, no siree, I always woke up with a hope and a plan, new adventures, new possibilities, always somethin' new."

Animated by his own conversation, Mac pulled himself up onto the fallen cedar. He kicked slowly at the moss on the rock at his feet, slowly scraping the rock bare, legs swinging like a young boy daydreaming the time away. "Yeah, I had a hard time sittin' still, fuckin A."

Buck watched the wasted old boy sitting and swinging his thoughts, miles away.

After a long time, a time filled with silent thinking, thinking that was soothed and broke open a little by the duet of distant waters rushing and winds whistling high in the trees, Buck took a turn.

"I'm just learning to walk away I guess," Buck submitted.

"For most of my life success was the thing. I never was able to fulfill the big ambitions, you know, running for president, owning a huge ranch in Wyoming, those kinds of things. But I did okay. I was comfortable being in charge of things, always moved in that direction. It seemed that in most situations, where the majority of folks work hard not to stick their necks out, I would. It didn't seem to bother me, and so a lot of times I'd end up ahead." Buck rubbed the back of his neck and stretched out his legs. "And I was a pretty good talker, but I'm not sure that was all of it either. I was a believer, maybe that was it, I believed in things like integrity and honor." Buck paused, struggling to put his thoughts into words, "I think that part of it was that I just didn't care about a lot of things other people worry about. I didn't really care deeply about how people felt about me."

Buck leaned forward to take a sip of the hot coffee, his wool socks stiff and soiled and wiggling back at him as he stretched his feet.

"You're so full of shit," Mac snorted, standing up and stepping closer to Buck. Buck looked up at him, surprised at his words.

Mac stood right in front of him, his barrel chest pushed out.

"You got all your precious thoughts and feelings, I've seen your type, and I'm guessing that you LOVE people fawning over you. You LOVE being the boss-man that everybody looks up to. I'm thinking you care more about the way people feel about you than any other single thing. 'I don't care what people think,' what a load of crap." Mac paused, momentarily running out of steam. He was silent for a minute then continued, "I've seen your type before, big, successful; buy what you want types, guys that just aren't capable of admitting that they're manipulative, self important greedy bastards who are just good at workin' people. I bet you've been doin' it all your life. You're one of those guys who always has to paint some phony picture about being honorable and concerned about doing the right thing when you're really just taking care of ol' number one. I'm thinkin' you don't need to learn nothin' 'bout walkin' away either. Guys like you walk away from anything that matters. All that spoutin' off last night 'bout your dear wife and your lovely kids, I don't see 'em here Bucko, don't see 'em hangin' out with their old man. You probably spent so much time worryin' about your own shit that they moved on an' you just haven't figured it out."

Mac sat back down and spat on the ground.

"So what is your real story, counselor?" Mac challenged.

"Wanna be a weekend mountain man?"

"Trying to find yourself?"

Mac raised his gray and skewed eyebrows in question, his mouth twisted in a scornful smile. A come-here-and-we'll-mix-it-up-asshole smile.

Buck stood up. He could feel himself backing away, moving from the conflict as he always had.

Mac reached out and threw another log on the fire, watching.

Buck began to turn away then stopped and faced Mac.

"I'm not walkin' away now."

Mac sat before him, returning his stare.

"Don't 'pear to be."

"I'm not sure why you need to be such an ass-hole."

Mac just looked at him and shrugged, then stared down at the fire. Buck looked away from Mac, looking at nothing. His eyes started to water, and he wiped them with his sleeve then walked a few paces from the camp, facing the ground they had already covered.

After a time he heard Mac clear his throat.

"You don' mind me, boyo, I say a lotta things, don' necessarily mean 'em."

Buck didn't respond.

After another pause, Mac sighed then spoke again. "Well, anyways, we got some ground to cover." Mac bent and rolled his bag and gear, swung the pack to his back and started hiking out of camp on a trail leading up towards a ridgeline on the right.

Buck pulled his gear together, tossed his coffee and the grounds from the pot and shoved the utensils into his pack. "Goddamn, weird old bastard," he mumbled to himself as he watched Mac disappear around a twist in the path, then hurried to follow.

Mac and Buck had only been walking an hour or so when Mac stopped and held up one hand.

"Do you feel it?" he asked, and Buck, starting to shake his head, hesitated, then quickly looked back into the woods.

"Like something's watching us?" he whispered.

"You got it boyo," Mac whispered back and peered intently into the trees, watching, then adjusting just a bit, studying each section of forest, watching for movement. Both of them were silent and still.

After a moment, Mac broke the silence. "Well, whatever it is, it's not showing itself, probably a bear." And after taking one more look, he turned and again headed up the trail, now winding steadily up towards the mountain.

Buck called after him, "Grizzly? Is that what you think?" Mac just threw up his hands and kept walking. After another hour or so they came to the top of the ridge that overlooked a small stream still filled with rushing water from a spring higher up. Right next to the stream was a makeshift camp. Lucky, hatless, was squatting beside the fire, his red hair and the darker black-brown stain on his forehead clearly visible. Just past him, head buried in the bear grass, was Buck's donkey.

Lucky looked up.

"Heard you last night," he tipped his head back and wo-wooed, grinning.

"That's some ugly wolves."

Lucky gestured towards some rocks circling the fire. "Have a seat. I figured you'd be coming along so I've been cookin'." He reached and turned a stick skewered with clumps of meat, dripping and sizzling over the fire as Mac and Buck lowered their packs to the ground.

"Caught some rabbit, all by myself," he said, looking up at Buck, their eyes connecting briefly.

Then Lucky turned to Mac, "You damn near dropped me off that cliff old man." Mac grinned in response.

"When I came to I couldn't find you anywhere, so I snuck back up top and grabbed the donkey and took off. I figured it would be safer up in the mountains."

Lucky nodded to Buck, "You got some fine gear mister," then standing up he held out his hand, "I'm Lucky, or not, but that's what I'm called."

Buck reached out and grasped his hand, calloused and strong.

"Buck," he responded, looking over at the donkey, "She okay?"

"Oh, yeah, she's just fine, great ol' donkey. We've just been getting acquainted."

They dropped each other's hand. Lucky glanced at Mac and back again to Buck. "Sorry about that robbery stuff, one of those nights I guess." He carefully touched the wound on his head.

Buck nodded. "Yeah, one of those nights, that's for sure."

Lucky turned and squatted next to the fire, adjusting the spit, then pointed down the far side of the ridge. "I think a couple of ladies are coming this way. One of them's that girlfriend of yours Mac boy," he said, raising his voice to a falsetto.

Buck looked at Mac, who gave Lucky a fierce glare. "Keep your eye on the rabbits, we don't want 'em burnt," Mac growled, then he turned and walked to the edge of the rock face where he could see further down the valley. He saw two small people, slowly moving up the ridge line towards them, the faint sound of laughter rising up to where Mac stood holding his hat in his hand, his perpetual scowl softening.

Well, I'll be, he thought.

CHAPTER FIVE

Are we all met? ₅

Anna sat on a curb in Butte at the corner of 3rd and Main Street at 1:30 in the morning. She was hungry. The baby inside of her gave her hunger a ravenous edge, filling her with a reckless need as she sat there big bellied in the cold and wet, shivering in the wind. She was running out of options and she knew it. Depressed and scared, she sat on that damp curb, wishing she could do something to kill the pain for just a little while.

Headlights approached, blinding her for a moment then slowing down and coming to a stop in front of her, tires sucking the damp rain from the streets. Anna, her hair dripping wet, looked up at the bent and rusted pickup. The passenger door swung open and a young man and his buddy, both gripping the necks of their beers, leaned out over each other.

"Hey there honey, we're two lonely cowboys lookin' to warm you up," the dark one shouted, laughing and pushing at his friend. "Why don't you hop on in here," he yelled, swinging the door all the way open. Anna looked blankly up at the drunken boys and abruptly pulled open her coat to reveal her belly swelling against a thin t-shirt.

"Been there done that, cowboy," Anna said in a hoarse voice, finding herself near tears. She bowed her head and stared down at the puddle surrounding her feet and heard the door slam and the truck move slowly away, the cowboys hooting and yelling as the engine raced. Her tears began to flow and mingle with the rain. Cold rain and warm tears falling on her taut belly, and her child restless and stirring within her.

After a time, Anna pushed herself up and walked toward the market. The market was going to be her salvation for now. The market already was a part of her descent into one of those cold empty places she tried not to examine to closely. Anna quickly glanced over her shoulder then entered an alley next to the store. The box boy whose favor she'd won earlier that day was waiting, clearly nervous, stepping from foot to foot. Anna avoided his eyes, trying to block her most recent nightmare.

Focus on his hands, focus on the key, she thought with desperation. "Look at the key, that's food for us, we gotta have that food honey." Talking now to her unborn child, ignoring the image of her humiliation, her trembling form, perched on her knees in that broken down Ford full of junk and empty souls. She touched her stomach. "We're going to eat baby, I promise you, I promise you that," she whispered fiercely as she watched the boy insert his key into the lock. When he turned the doorknob, she brushed past him, pushed open the door, and hurried into the shop. It was dark, lit only by the display case lights and green exit signs on the walls. She grabbed a plastic bag and began filling it with meats and cheese and cans then ran outside, ran down the street holding her food with one hand and grasping her stomach with the other.

◆ ◆ ◆ ◆

The rabbits were burning and spitting over the fire. Buck was brushing Bob-a-Lou, unpacking and repacking his gear. Buck noticed at some point that Mac had disappeared, and when he returned he was glowing, pink faced and shirtless. His belly, freed of his shirt and coat, dropped, hairy and white over his belt. He rubbed his face with damp hands then pushed back his hair, combing it with his gnarled fingers.

Lucky looked at Buck and shook his head. He reached out and carefully lifted the skewered meat from the fire then set it on a nearby chunk of bluestone, licking his fingers where he had touched the roasted meat.

"Got some grease with winter coming."

Buck had been pulling a wire brush over Bob-a-Lou's head and neck when his attention was snared by the sight of Mac's enormous gut. Distracted, he dragged the wire brush over one of the donkey's ears. Bob-a-Lou jerked back then turned and bit Buck's hand, hard. Buck shouted in pain and the donkey brayed then kicked a piece of wood into the fire scattering sparks and ash. Mac just stood there, mouth open in surprise at the commotion, both hands holding the underside of his belly as he leaned back from the fray. At that moment, Sister Toni rounded a granite boulder and stood before them.

Toni turned to Jesse, her eyes smiling.

"This is why I've chosen to live my life without a man." Toni gestured with her walking stick to Mac's massive belly and then pointed to Buck, bent over his hand, his face anguished and tight.

"This one," she said, turning to Lucky as he relocated the skewer of rabbit on a flat rock further from the fire, jabbing again with her walking stick, "This one might make a good handyman, with some training."

Mac started to sputter and Toni just smiled at him. "Go get dressed. You look," she paused, "Clean."

"Yes ma'am." Mac mumbled and hustled off behind some trees. Toni turned back to the fire.

"You must be Lucky." Toni placed both hands together on top of her staff, looking at Lucky as if he were the only interest she had on the mountain that day. "Mac's told me a lot about you. He's quite proud of your skill as a woodsman." Lucky grinned and stared at the ground and then looked up again at Toni, then at Jesse, wondering who she was.

"And who are you, man who just was bitten by a donkey?" Buck sighed, "My name's Buck, ma'am."

Nodding her head, Toni responded, "This is Jesse, my charge. I assume, since you've been standing here staring at us for the better part of an hour, that we're invited for supper. Lucky, why don't you and Jesse get things laid out and I'll attend to Mr. Buck's hand." Toni grabbed Buck's arm and told him to sit. She set down her pack and started digging for her doctoring kit.

Buck, following directions, sat down and looked at her.

"You always this bossy?"

"I prefer being in charge; works better, takes less time." She pulled a glass bottle of something out of her kit and twisted off the lid. Mac came back into view, mumbling, "She's a control freak, just like you, talked me into climbin' on the wagon once for longer than I care to think about." Toni smiled and rolled Buck's hand towards her, frowning at the half circle of tooth marks, now bleeding and starting to bruise.

"Yes, that was a long three days MacMillan." "For all of us," she added as she poured part of the contents of the bottle directly on the wound. Buck stiffened and fought to hold back another scream. Toni turned to Mac, "Rubbing alcohol, it will kill you quicker than what you usually drink, so stay away from it." Mac just looked at her and shook his head.

After they finished eating the rabbit and washing it down with water cool from the creek, Toni asked, "Lucky, what happened to your head?"

"I got myself shot, ma'am."

"When?"

"Well," Lucky looked uncomfortably at the ground and then at Mac, who just shrugged and sat back.

"May as well tell her kid, one of our finer moments."

Buck glanced over at Mac then Lucky, wondering about the kid that was killed and the violence that must be simmering under Lucky's easy manner.

"Well you see, Mac and me we were sitting up by the pass, there's a cliff near the top that looks down at the highway, and we sometimes sit and drink and make up stuff about the cars going by."

Jesse asked, "Make up stuff?"

"Yeah, you know, like we'll see a new Hummer go by and maybe see a guy in the dash lights and I'll say, 'You know, I bet that bucko just left his squeeze down on the Moyie River and is heading home to a wife that doesn't appreciate him and he's expecting trouble. He's probably too drunk to be driving and is wishing that he had one more cold beer before he had to face the music. And Mac will say, 'Nah, that's just some environmental wacko heading over to Glacier to protest global warming, probably left his suburban at home, plans to cozy up to some high-strung tree hugger lookin' for love, phony asshole.' You know stuff like that."

Lucky smiled, looking unsuccessfully at Toni and Jesse for confirmation. "Well anyway, Mac built us a seat from bluestone. Lucky stopped again at their blank stares. "It's real comfy, you know, for sittin' up there," he added.

Sister Toni gave Mac an amused look, "Lots of time on your hands, eh Mac?"

"Get on with it Lucky," Mac said.

"Anyway, we were sitting there and this old truck and trailer slides over the center of the road heading straight for a big semi. The semi's horn blasts and we jumped up and all hell breaks loose. The truck swerved to the right, trailer swinging, just missing the semi. We could hear a donkey braying."

Lucky glanced at Buck, "We thought it was a mule, but Buck here he set us straight, anyway, the truck slowed down and pulled over in the gravel on the side of the road. It was pretty exciting you know, all that sound and confusion. We hooted and yelled a bit and watched ol' Buck here crawl out of the cab and check his donkey, then one of us got the bright idea to get our hands on that donkey. Buck here 'peared to be all alone and kind of vulnerable, sorry Buck," Lucky added, looking over at Buck and Bob-a-Lou. "So we snuck on down, and Buck, he got out of the truck right on cue and walked right into Mac's gun. Well then, just when we were going to take Bob-a-Lou here I done got shot." Lucky shrugged, "Took a chunk right out of the top of my head."

"Lucky," Sister Toni questioned, "I don't understand, did Buck shoot you?"

"Oh no, he wouldn't have done that, his gun was still in the saddle bags."

Sister Toni persisted, a little impatiently, "Mac shot you?"

"Jesus Christ, Sister." Mac exploded and at her sharp look he amended, "I mean jees, you know I'd never hurt Lucky."

"Well?" she responded.

Lucky and Mac looked at each other, then at Buck who took a step back.

"Not my story."

Finally Mac spoke. "You see Lucky got mixed up in a little something with the McLaren boy, the troublesome one," he added.

"Mac, that boy was killed."

"Yeah, that's the truth," Mac said, and continued, "Now before you get all judgmental there were 'stenuating circumstances. You tell 'em Lucky."

Lucky stood before the group, clearly uncomfortable, then sat down and picked up a twig and started snapping off small pieces.

He paused, itched at his ear, and said, "Things go back a ways. Ian, that was his name, Ian's been known for hurting kids for some time now, you know, messing with them. I'd heard about it but it wasn't till a couple of months ago that I seen things first hand. A lady from over in Idaho came up to me at the Tavern and asked me to help find her son. He was only ten years old. She'd heard about my trackin' 'bilities, I guess. She knew where her son was last seen, up in the Spread Creek drainage where they were huckleberryin'. She needed help so I went an' helped her.

"The sign was pretty clear, less than a day old, and we worked our way up an old logging road and found them at an abandoned cabin down near the creek. The two of them were inside. Ian must have been right in the middle of it. When I kicked opened the door, Ian was standing there with a rifle and not much else on and the boy was lying in the dirt. I'm not sure what happened next. I thought Ian moved the barrel towards me, but maybe not, but anyway I shot him and he died quick enough." Lucky stopped, picked up another twig, and continuing to break off small pieces, started to talk again.

"I hauled Ian down to his Pa for buryin' and left him at the ranch. Old McLaren must have figured it out. Figured out that I did it I mean."

Lucky stopped talking and they all sat without saying anything. Their quiet thoughts settled uneasily with the silence of the place as the sun worked its way off the shelf.

It started to get cold.

Finally, Sister Toni got up and threw some more wood on the fire. "Sometimes things happen and there's no right or wrong in it." Glancing up at Mac she continued, "This needs to be dealt with Mac, now, not later. McLaren will know soon enough that Lucky's alive."

"Prob'ly already knows. Kep' shootin' after Lucky fell. Must a' known he din't finish the job."

Toni squared off and faced Mac, her concern now clearly etched on her face. She spoke slowly, emphasizing each word. "This young boy is your ward. You might start fulfilling your obligations by not running around in the woods, drunk and delirious, always dragging Lucky along, and take some steps to protect him."

Angry now, Sister Toni stared at Mac, who looked away and into the cold flames of the fire. Eventually he began to speak.

"Sister, I'm not sure what I can do about it. I'm sure as hell not turning Lucky in for anything. I can't hurt ol' man McLaren, God knows he's been through it." Mac turned from the fire and addressed Toni directly. "You're right about the drinkin' and carousing. Don't know if I can do anything about that either, been with me for a long time." He raised his voice a little. "Lots of things hiding behind that bottle, not sure I can face 'em bare, you know."

Lucky stood up, breaking the pall the conversation had cast on all of them. "Hell, I'm okay Sister, pardon the language, things work out." He stopped for a moment and looked over at Mac.

"It's getting' cold and I'm going to rustle up some wood for the night."

Lucky took a step away from the fire, "Come on Jesse, let's leave these old folks to ponder the meaning of life." Jesse, surprised, grinned and said "You got it," and the two of them headed up the ridge to collect wood, talking quietly, Jesse once glancing back at Sister Toni.

"So what are you doing here?" Buck asked Sister Toni, who responded by sitting down on the rock next to Mac, patting him on the arm as she sat, apologizing a little for her harsh words.

"Well, I guess you would say that Jesse and I are on a quest. She's an orphan, no mom or dad that I can find. I found her when she ran away from a foster home down in Troy, a bad one, and spent the night curled up in an old blanket at the edge of my pasture. She's only got one thing out of the past that she holds onto and that's a story that someone, she thinks it was her mom, would tell her as a young child before she would go to bed. At night, that's when she tells the story to the children, she lights up with hope, and I can't help but feel that God is directing me to make that story real if I can. Making it real involves climbing this mountain." As she concluded, she looked towards the peak rising above them, now capturing the setting sun. The golden tamarack and aspen contrasting with the deep green of the fir and the gray black of the bare trees and the rock face of the summit. All of it was framed by a firmament of deepening blue sky.

"God's home," Toni stated quietly.

Buck sat and watched the fire slowly climbing the newly added logs. Lucky and Jesse were moving in and out of the trees, bending then standing as they collected firewood. Buck thought of the last few hours, sitting on this shelf, interacting with these people. He was enormously comfortable for no good reason. He could feel the beginning chill of days end on his hands and face. Bob-a-Lou poked her head next to him and the damp warmth of the donkey's breath and the damp cold of the wind slowly sliding off the mountain caressed his skin and swirled his unkempt hair. He thought about Mac and Lucky, about Mac protecting Lucky. It was a problem without a solution that appeared both crucial and pressing, even alarming, but at the same time seemed to be a part of the rhythms of the woods and the hills. As if a resolution had already been defined, but not yet discovered.

"Do you really believe that God has asked you to go on this quest?" he asked Toni.

"Do you talk to God, Buck," Sister Toni responded.

Buck thought for a moment. "I've tried, never had much luck."

"How did it feel?"

"I don't know. Sometimes when I'd try to pray there would be a fleeting sense of warmth or comfort, of affirmation. I'm not sure that I trust my feelings all that much, though. I've been wrong enough over the years."

"What else you got, Bucko?" Mac asked. "You can't trust your feelings, hell, that's all that's real. Words are bullshit. People sure can't be trusted. I don't know about God, but all this," and he threw out his hands, "All of this, I feel. I feel it so hard it sometimes rocks me to the core. I get all shrunk down and fold into every creek and draw and slam into every rock face and it all screams at me, 'This is real! This right here, right now, is real!' I sure as hell trust that." He paused for a moment looking from Buck to Toni then continued, "So if you don't have that what else do y' got?"

Buck sat back and thought about it. He couldn't come up with much of an answer. The only time he felt the deep down core-rocking feeling that Mac was describing was when he drank too much or had something scare the bejesus out of him. He recognized that he was more prone to be detached, more loosely connected to people and events. Things didn't scream at him, not like that. But as he rested, tasting the fragrance of the mountain and burnt pine and water-soaked stones, he realized that something new was happening to him. His surroundings were connecting directly to something inside him, stirring him, awakening him in a way he really didn't understand.

"You know Mac, I'm not sure what else you do have. I guess I just don't burn quite as fiercely as you do."

Sister Toni looked back at Buck. "To me God is here right now, in us, in the mountains. God is listening to our fears and wants and guiding us in his own way. We may not be capable of understanding him, but we can learn to listen, learn to hear His words, that's what I believe." Sister Toni broke eye contact with Buck and looked out at the steep hillside in the fading light then spoke once more.

"This quest is God's direction as best as I can understand it."

Mac stood up, out from under Sister Toni's hand that had been resting on his arm, and stomped over to the fire, kicking at the burning embers, dust and sparks rising from his boots. He glanced up the ridge where Jesse and Lucky had disappeared, then turned back to Sister Toni. "Well hells bells Sister, beggin' your pardon and all, I mean that's all fine and good. But just what is it exactly that God told you to do? Get up and climb a mountain? Drag this girl up into the woods and chase some bears? What the heck is your quest?"

Sister Toni looked up at Mac.

"You don't have to keep askin' my pardon Mac, I've listened to your tongue and a lot worse over the years."

Sister Toni's soft voice hardened a bit as she continued.

"I'm also not sure the exact details of my conversations with God are any of your business. But if you must know, I didn't have a vision or hear a voice talking in my head telling me to run all over the backcountry. I listened to a story told by a young woman, and I acted accordingly."

Sister Toni then retold Jesse's story of the Big Rock Candy Mountain, telling it as best she could. When she mentioned Bill Bungle, she noticed that Mac raised his head, eyes alive for a moment, then fading as Mac stared out over the same hillside as the others but saw a different place.

"I don't expect to find a secret valley of course, or a magic stream, but I think the glimmer of hope in this young women's eyes lays in that direction, so that's where I'm going."

The sun had disappeared from the mountain by the time Lucky and Jesse returned with loads of sticks and logs and laughter. Sister Toni looked at Mac. "It looks like the magic is already happening, doesn't it." But Mac didn't respond, he just looked out at the darkening hills, remembering a young girl full of life and trouble and lonely eyes and a story he used to listen to sitting around a campfire a long time ago.

CHAPTER SIX

Thy threats have no more strength
than her weak prayers. 6

It had been five months since she'd slipped. Her baby was just three years old and Anna had tried hard to face each morning with a clear head. If she woke before her daughter she would fall to her knees and bend over her hands at the side of the bed and pray. She would beg to be strong, to be there for her little girl. She prayed to push back the fear that ate away at her, the fear that always followed her hunger and loneliness and desperate yearning for companionship. Sometimes she would pray with her little girl beside her, listening to her small and wondering voice, thanking God for her mommy and her kitty and then looking up at Anna expectantly for approval. And then she'd ask for a story. "Please

Mommy a story?" And Anna always responded, "Okay honey, okay."

This morning, Anna felt a little thrill of anticipation as she got dressed. She had a day off from working at the restaurant. The girl downstairs had offered to babysit in the evening for a couple of hours. Anna had been watching the marquee at the club downtown for weeks. A live band was coming to town and she was going to listen to music, and dance, and oh God, it'd been a long time since she'd done that. Anna could feel that little nudge of anxiety when she thought of being out at a club, with boys and whiskey and her little girl back home, but she firmly pushed it back. I'll be fine, I deserve a night out, she told herself as her tension mingled with her happy expectations for the evening.

The day passed quickly and finally her babysitter arrived. After giving way too many instructions to the sitter, who didn't seem to be listening anyway, Anna gave her little girl a big hug, told her to be good, and ran down the stairs into the street.

When she arrived at the club at seven it was just as she had dreamed it would be. The guy at the door flirted with her and promised her a dance later. She sat at a small table close to the band and the music was loud and filled her head and tingled her spine and swung her legs and when the middle-aged waitress leaned over and asked, "Do you want a drink honey?" She ordered a coke and rum without missing a beat. And then her glass was empty and she ordered another and another and then she was dancing with a cowboy with a big hat and loud voice who whirled her around, pressing her up against his hard frame. Later she was sitting at a table with a group, laughing and tossing whiskey and dancing some more, and finally she walked out the door into the still night, the flush of the alcohol protecting her from the cold night air.

She was filled with bright lights and swirling snow and gay thoughts as she shuffled and sang her way back to her apartment. Turning the corner to her home, she saw a police car in front of her building. She started to run, and fell, hard. She was struggling to get up when she saw a woman in a uniform come out of her door, her little girl in the officer's arms. She staggered up, her arms reaching towards her child. "My baby, is she okay, what are your doing with my baby?" Another officer, a man, stepped in front of her and grabbed her shoulders.

"You leave a young child like this alone Ma'am, you're not fit. Not fit to care for her. Look at you! You're falling down drunk, for Christ's sake."

He shook his head in disgust, pushing her away.

"But I had a sitter, where's my sitter?" Anna rushed over and pounded with both hands on the door of the lower apartment. "Lisa, Lisa you have to tell them, Lisa, open up!" The police pulled her away from the door and held her as her daughter was being put into the car screaming, "Mommy! Mommy!" Anna could still hear her cry as the police car door slammed and the car pulled away, its tires crushing into the ice-covered gravel on the side of the road.

Anna sat on the steps, alone, sobbing. Her head was spinning, and then she was throwing up and finally she crawled up the stairs to her apartment and passed out on the floor.

She woke in the morning, stiff and stinking and confused, and then Anna remembered. She struggled to get up and wash, then walked to the police station, the only place she knew to go. The woman at the desk told her it was Saturday and no one could do anything to help her until Monday. She wandered through the town, thinking she might see her daughter, hoping but knowing it was hopeless, not knowing where to go or who to turn to, until finally it was time for her to go to work. After an hour of washing dishes she knew she couldn't do that anymore, and she pulled a couple of twenties from the till and walked back to the club and drank, and drank until she forgot it all.

◆ ◆ ◆ ◆

Morning broke softly on the mountain. Buck opened his eyes and saw a soft light beginning to fill the valley. Clouds had settled below the ridge where they had slept, a white lake of clouds, stretching all the way to the massive ridges to the south and east. The sky above was equally covered, gray and dense, the top of the mountain hidden from view. Buck could see Sister Toni sitting on the edge of the ridge, gazing over the low clouds. She and the morning were still and silent. Just down the hill, Buck could barely make out the form of Bob-a-Lou, head down in the grass, her light gray coat blending with the mist.

Lying on his side, warm in his bag, Buck remembered the solemn pact made in the dark, in the light of the dwindling fire. "To the mountain!" he and Lucky had toasted with coffee in their metal cups, entranced with Jesse and Sister Toni and their adventure. As they toasted he remembered watching Jesse huddle against Lucky. Jesse's eyes were wary, uncertain, unsure of her company. Just before Buck had lain his head down to sleep he had also seen Sister Toni in the quavering shadows and the dark, sitting beside Mac, cupping her coffee with both hands, her eyes seemingly on Jesse, her body leaning lightly against Mac's rough clothes.

Now, reluctant to move from the warmth and comfort of his bed Buck rested with his sleeping bag pulled up over his shoulders. He wondered about Jesse's life and the struggles she had encountered and her tale of the Rock Candy Mountain. He was not familiar with the story she told but he had, for as long as he could remember, fantasized about the Big Rock Candy Mountain. He had read the poem as a boy. In his mind, it was a place of men and magic and desperate hope. Until he recently discovered the mountain on a map he had not thought of it as something real, just a place that was very different and far from his current circumstance. In his youth he would spend long hours in the back seat of the family station wagon, driving with his parents through the mountains. He would peer up at the tops of ridges and summits, yearning to explore, wondering if the Big Rock Candy Mountain was somewhere up there past the steep slopes and granite cliffs, waiting for him. It had been a fiction, like Jesse's mountain, that now was very real for both of them.

Finally, Buck folded back his bag, pulling it over his legs and stood up. Sister Toni walked up the slope towards him, stopped, brushed her hands against the front of her coat, and looked at Buck.

"Mac's gone."

"What do you mean? Where'd he go?"

"I'm not sure," Toni answered. She turned away and looked at the spot where Mac had bedded down. "He and his gear, they're just gone. He's like that sometimes, moves on before the glue sticks."

They were both silent for a moment, Buck watching Toni's still back, thinking of reaching out, touching her shoulder, feeling a hint of her sadness, but then Toni walked away to roust the others, shaking bags and rubbing faces, calling out to the morning. "Come on gang, let's go climb this dang mountain."

Jessie asked where Mac had gone, if they were sure he was all right.

"That's just his way," Lucky responded.

As they broke camp, Buck found he was anxious, uncertain about being in the woods without Mac. He carefully loaded the pack onto Bob-a-Lou. When he stood up after tightening the cinch he sensed that someone or something was watching him. It was the same feeling that he and Mac had experienced the day before. He could feel his gut tightening as he turned and looked into the woods, looking for movement but seeing nothing.

Twenty minutes later, they were on the trail. Instead of fading away, the mass of clouds below slowly followed them up the hill until they finally combined with the gray sky above, turning their world into a place of soft light and gray-black shadows. The path they were following was fairly straight, bordered by the shadowy outline of trees and brush and rising steadily upward. Lucky and Jesse took the lead, followed by Sister Toni. Buck brought up the rear with Bob-a-Lou.

Buck heard something crashing through the underbrush to the left of the trail and stopped to listen, his heart racing. He stood quietly, waiting for the sound to reoccur, but there was only silence and a whisper of wind, high overhead.

They continued upward. Growing tired and struggling with the steepness of the path, Buck steadily fell behind, stopping often to catch his breath and rest his legs. Sister Toni would occasionally call ahead to slow Jesse and Lucky then wait for Buck to close the gap.

The trail flattened out for a few feet and Buck stopped. To his right he thought he saw the dark reflection of water. He hesitated, looking around for a moment. The forest just off the trail was dense, small trees woven with berries and twisting vines. A narrow path led to the glimpse he'd had of water, further in. Shaking off a growing sense of apprehension, he stepped off the trail to explore. After just a few steps he came across a spring seeping from the side of the hill. It fed a small pond that was perched on a shelf of cedar and berries. He pulled Bob-a-Lou over and let her drink. As he stood and listened to the donkey's slurping and the rising wind, the hairs on the back of his neck literally began to stand on end. He started to turn to look behind him when the donkey abruptly raised her head and wide-eyed pulled back on the lead, backing from the pond. Buck looked at the donkey, then at the water, and noticed a print, just to the right of his boot. Five claws marks crowned the print, which was wider and longer than his foot.

Buck froze, his heart pounding. He looked up and realized that he could no longer see Sister Toni or the others. He peered into the fog and clouds then felt dampness on his check. Snow began to fall and swirl in front of him. He stood unmoving as the snowfall increased and the route up the mountain quickly disappeared. Finally, his fear broke his paralysis. He yanked Bob-a-Lou's reins and stumbled out towards the trail.

After just a few steps Buck stopped. He could hear the rising whistle and moan of the wind and the sharp cracks and growls of the frozen tamaracks as they bent and twisted. Suddenly the snow was so thick he couldn't see the ground before him. He remembered that water had cut a deep rivulet in the middle of the path they had been following and he reached out with his boot to locate it. Finally finding the narrow crevice, he began to step upwards, head now bent against the snow, heart beating, listening carefully for sounds of the bear.

Buck hurriedly climbed the trail. His exhaustion was pushed back by his panic. He realized that any comfort or sense of tranquility he had experienced on the mountain had disappeared. He was surrounded by something alien and indifferent, something frightfully wild. Trying to stifle his fear, he forced himself to think about his companions, about finding them up ahead. His companions! Shit! He realized that in the last moments, from the time he had first felt the overwhelming presence of the bear, he hadn't tried to alert the others. Now he called out, "Sister Toni, Lucky!" But his words were snatched by the growing winds as quickly as he could utter them. He kept pushing upwards, pulling the donkey behind him, looking back into the snow and shadows, seeing the dark outlines of a grizzly everywhere. Suddenly, a hand appeared from his left and grabbed him. He yelled out, alarmed and started to pull away, but felt the grip on his arm tighten and heard Lucky's voice.

"It's okay, Bucko, just us chickens. Now duck in here, we'll wait the storm out."

Buck, his breath ragged, too recently frightened to even respond, turned and pulled Bob-a-Lou behind him, following Lucky's blurred form into the darkness.

Buck could feel the rough granite against his glove on one side and dirt and tree roots on the other. He could no longer feel the wind on his face.

Huddled up against Lucky and Jesse, he felt the quick touch of Sister Toni's hand on his shoulder. He looked blankly at Lucky as Lucky held up his hand in caution, not understanding until he whispered.

"Quiet now, he's out there," gesturing into the storm then pressing the .44 into Buck's hand.

"Careful, it's loaded."

The four of them sat huddled together.

Jesse could feel the cold start to inch into her boots and her side that wasn't pressed against Sister Toni. The driving snow was so thick it seemed as if night had fallen. She could feel the breath of the donkey as it leaned into her, away from the cut of the wind. The donkey smelled of dirt and sweat, its breath sweet and cloying.

Jesse was a little afraid but at least she knew she wasn't alone. She'd been alone a lot before, before she met Sister Toni. There were times when she had been on the streets when she had no one to help her push back her fears. By herself, she had no choice but to focus on surviving each moment, trying to get through to another day. She wasn't nearly as afraid now as she had been when the bodies of other kids had been pressed against her, smelling of whiskey and the sweet pungent odor of weed, all of them huddled together in the window well of a building on a dark street, huddled for warmth, huddled to survive, waiting out the snow and wind, the night;

watching fearfully for anyone who might roust them out into those cold streets; waiting for the hands resting on her shoulders to become more purposeful, forcing her back into the cold, afraid she might not be able to break free if they groped her, afraid she might not want to break free.

No, it wasn't as bad as those times. Things were going to be okay now.

"It's okay." She had told her mom the last time they spoke in the dark, echoing hall of the court-house. Her mom, all skinny and crying, asking her, "Oh, honey, are you sure you're alright?" Her mom, standing in front of her, her head shaking like she was old, holding her hands together before her belly, plump with poison.

"I'm so sorry, I tried, I really tried," she had cried, then pushed towards Jesse, her arms reaching out to touch her, to grasp her coat, to touch her hair.

"They said this was best for you; tell me it's best for you, please honey!"

Jesse had felt her Mom's trembling hands, looked into her hungry eyes, and couldn't respond, couldn't say anything as her stomach twisted and hurt. She didn't understand. Panic consumed her as her mom insisted, "You're going to be okay, things will be fine," already pulling back, stepping away, glancing towards the door. As Jesse watched her Mom pull her worn overcoat over her wasted frame and turn and walk away, she felt the world hardening around her, preventing her from feeling anything. She watched her Mom leaning with her whole body against the massive courthouse doors, not looking back, just pushing one door open and slipping through. Jesse had stood on the hardwood floor of the courthouse, all alone, tears running down her cheeks, feeling nothing, staring at the closed doors where her Mom had disappeared. And now Lucky was reaching over and gently wiping the tears that were freezing onto her face, melting them with the touch of his hands.

"Don't cry now kiddo, it's only a storm, I've been through wors'n this a lot."

Sister Toni wrapped Jesse's chin and face with her scarf. "Sit next to me now and cuddle up, it won't last long." And she and Lucky held Jesse between them. And just like that Jesse felt better, colder than hell and scary as could be, but fine with the world at that moment.

Sister Toni silently prayed to her God to hold them all in the hollow of His hand. Her prayers seemed weak and puny before the wind and the cold, but her faith felt as strong and mighty as the storm itself. She watched Lucky's shadowy form move from Jesse's side and start to chop away at the ground. Buck was using one hand to push Bob-a-Lou to the side, trying to give Lucky room to work. They both pulled moss and twigs from the trees in front of them and put them together into a pile for a fire, down low and out of the wind.

◆ ◆ ◆ ◆

By dawn, Mac had crossed the east face of the mountain, staying just above the tree line. He stopped on a clear slope above the edge of the woods and sat against the hillside to watch the sun rise over a mountain range deep within the Rockies. The jagged peaks were slowly defined by the light, first black and sharp against the sky then fading to shades of gray, softened and diffused by the early sun and the valley mists. To the north, he could see a dark mass of clouds pushing towards him.

Mac's certainty and purpose, so clear when he had awoke in the night and left Sister Toni a scrawled note, wavered when he stopped and the morning came alive around him. It was the beginning of his second day without drink and Mac savored the clear, sharp scent of daybreak and the brightness of the sun. He was struck by a physical rush of wellbeing, not filtered or diluted. He raised his arms to the sun and pushed out his feet, feeling the burn and stretch of his leg muscles as they tightened and re-laxed. God, it was times like this that he wondered why he ever drank, why he ever did anything to sep-arate himself from the intensity of this glorious world. He smiled, thinking that he was starting to sound like Toni, thinking that maybe it is God's time to talk to folks, mornings like this. He looked up and raised his voice. "So is that you God?" His voice called out to the forests and echoed off the rock peaks far above. "You the one who put all these fool notions in my head?" he challenged, then waited in silence, waiting for an answer in the warmth of the sun now touching the slope where he rested. He thought about the note he left in the pocket of Toni's cloak and wondered about Toni reading that note. He patted the smooth rock next to him and smiled thinking of the way Toni had squealed and swung at him when he patted her firm little behind. He just smiled and soaked up the sun for a bit.

A while later, after the clouds rolled in and the sun disappeared, the warmth leaving with it, Mac leaned forward, away from the hill, grunted and stood up, his back to the mountain, head up, shoulders back, "Tits out," as his Pa used to say. He stood quietly for a moment, paying tribute to all that surrounded him then grabbed his pack with one hand and moved quickly down through the trees. A few minutes later it began to snow.

◆ ◆ ◆ ◆

The snow kept falling and blowing into the small cavity where Buck and the others huddled together. The cold pushed inward, its progress slowed only a little by the small burning fire and the warmth of the donkey pressed against them. Buck knew that he was on the side of a massive mountain with a vista overlooking hundreds of miles of forest. But he could not quite grasp that knowledge or reconcile that thought with their small cramped and darkened space, defined only by the howl of the wind and the dark swirling snows, a space that extended no further than the huddled bodies around him. The fire was starting to fail. Lucky had pulled or tore from the ground all the loose fuel he could find in their particular hollow. When Buck quietly asked if one of them should go out and collect some wood, Lucky silently shook his head, his hands holding his rifle ready, its barrel pulled back and away from the snow.

Lucky kept staring into the dark as if he could sense something in the turmoil surrounding them, looking left then right, slowly, hands opening and closing on the rifle stock and magazine. Sister Toni and Jesse were all but invisible, huddled under their cloaks and tucked in behind the donkey's hindquarters, silent and frozen in place and in time.

Buck could no longer feel his toes or fingertips. The thin leather grocery store gloves were stiff and provided little protection. The pitch of the wind was unchanging. The passage of time was measured only by the slow invasion of the cold as it penetrated dee-per into his limbs and torso, and the build-up of snow drifting and sticking to their coats and gear. Buck's face and forehead were stiff with cold, ice frosting his three-day-old whiskers. The cold hurt. That's good, he thought. Good to hurt. He'd read that when things quit hurting you were in trouble. He couldn't remember where he'd learned that, some-where, he remembered that, not sure where. He be-gan to shiver, his eyes starting to close. His head fell lower, nodding towards his chest. Lucky reached out and pushed at him then pushed again. Buck looked up and saw Lucky holding his gloved hand to his fro-zen lips, gesturing with his head towards the snow and dark.

"It's ending," he whispered, "Keep a watch."

As the snowfall thinned Buck began to see the definition of the roots of a massive pine tree uprooted in a pile of dirt and rocks directly in front of them on the downside slope. Beyond this he could make out the outline of the trees standing thick in all directions. He began to see color, just a hint of green then finally the rich blue green of the evergreens contrasting with the yellow fall colors, and, as the last flakes fell to the ground he could see the stark blue of the sky, brilliant and clean against the new white snow.

Lucky held up his hand to caution Buck and the ladies as they pulled aside hoods and blankets and slowly stood. Bob-a-Lou snorted and moved out of the small alcove, nibbling at the still green limbs of a berry bush she had found at the edge of the granite.

Lucky cautiously stepped back towards the pathway, carefully examining the ground below the trail, his finger resting on the trigger. He slowly turned in a complete circle. He looked once again at the donkey, calmly now pawing aside the snow to get to the grass below, then lowered his rifle and broke the stillness.

"Well, I guess he's moved on." Lucky said, looking at Sister Toni and Jesse standing close together, then at Buck stamping his feet and clapping his frozen hands.

"Who moved on?" asked Jesse, shivering, and holding tight to Sister Toni. Toni answered, giving Lucky a stern look. "Just a bear, just an old bear we've seen round the mountain."

Toni reached out and gathered her cloak around her and Jesse.

"Lucky, you'd better warm up that fire unless you want to cart two frozen women down to the valley."

Lucky grabbed a hand-ax from Bob-a-Lou's pack and looked at Buck, "Let's break up some wood. This is as good a place for a camp as any."

Soon the fire was warming both the party and the rocks behind them. Lucky had boiled some water and made a beef broth to drink. With the storm gone, the mountains to the west were softly tinted in red and orange by the setting sun. They all had thawed their frozen limbs in front of the fire and were warmed and fed. Buck and Jesse were joking about Buck falling behind and not being able to keep up with the rest, and Buck was explaining his need to meditate as he climbed to "maximize the experience."

"Sounds like way too much bullshit to me, Buck," Lucky observed. He was standing, rifle in hand, looking out over the silent woods.

"Yeah it's mostly bullshit alright," Buck responded.

Jesse laughed, her eyes dancing with light when she smiled. Buck and Lucky were incapable of doing anything but smile back. The three were feeling pretty good. They had faced the elements and survived, high spirits buoyed by their youth and inexperience.

Sister Toni was staring into the flickering blue flames and quietly feeding the small fire. "You know, we're warm here," Lucky said. "The summit's only a half-hour away but there's no shelter once we leave the forest, only alpine firs that don't stand so high and rocks, lots of rocks. I'm thinkin' we should settle in for the night and make the last push in the morning. Give us plenty of time to get down the mountain, prob'ly night over at your place Sister, if that's alright." Lucky looked over at Buck, then Toni, a question in his eyes. Buck followed his gaze over to Sister Toni and saw her nodding in agreement as she reached into her pocket, looking down as if she had discovered something. She pulled out a piece of paper, folded over. Unfolding it, she looked up at the others.

"It's a note from Mac. He must have put in into my cloak before he left." Toni looked back down and was quiet, intent on reading. Suddenly she looked up, a horrified look on her face.

"Oh no! Oh my God, no! What have I done?"

Her whole body seemed to slump inward. The note was clutched in her shaking hands. With her eyes full of hurt and apology she glanced at Lucky then began to quietly read the note out loud.

Dear Sister:

I hope you won't feel the worse about me for what I plan to do. You see your concerns about Lucky are legit. He is my ward and I need to take care of him and this situation. I guess I've been running away from most everything all my life, including turning my back on that little girl's mother. Yes, I figured that out and 'spect you did too. McLaren's an old man who thinks he must avenge his son's dyin, probably won't stop till it's done. I'm an old guy too and I kinda understand McLaren. I'm pretty sure he would see the sense in making a trade. I'll probably get kilt by the bottle soon anyway. I know you think I can beat the drinkin but your God doesn't seem to work so well with me. Make my amends to Lucky. Help him see this as a thing I gotta do. Tell Buck he's got the makin's of a first rate tree rat.

You're a fine woman.

I remain

Forever yours,

MAC

"We have to stop him," Sister Toni said, her voice thin with panic. Lucky immediately jumped up and started throwing together a pack. Jesse and Buck followed suit and Buck asked, "What does it mean? What is Mac doing?"

"He's sacrifizin' himself that dumb son of a bitch." Lucky answered.

With one arm in his pack and the rifle in his hand Lucky started to cross back to the trail then abruptly he stopped. He could hear something. A moment passed and then they all heard it. Trees and branches were snapping and crashing as if a man-size boulder was rolling towards them across the side of mountain. They heard a fierce barking and popping then a deep guttural roar. Lucky cried, "Jesus Christ!" He dropped his pack and shouldered his rifle in one motion.

"Your gun!" Lucky screamed at Buck and then swung his rifle toward the red-brown mass hurtling towards them. Jesse cried out as Toni knocked her to the ground, pushing her into a shallow cut in the granite wall and the shelter exploded with the crescendo of the bear's roar and the rapid percussion of bullets as Lucky opened fire.

CHAPTER SEVEN

Now the hungry lion roars
And the wolf behowls the moon. 7

Buck looked up and everything slowed down. He saw Lucky swing his rifle towards the bear and he reached down to pull his .44 from his pack, clicking off the safety as he grabbed the butt of the gun. Lucky yelled and fired several shots, sharp cracks, lost in the bear's guttural roar and Jesse's scream. Then Buck saw Lucky's boots slip in the snow, his body bouncing against the gray granite and falling to the ground, directly in the path of the charging bear.

When the bear was only feet from Lucky's outstretched form, Sister Toni emerged from his right, a gray and black blur charging at the bear with her walking stick grasped in both hands like a spear. Without thinking, Buck jumped, knocking Sister Toni out of the way and then rolled back towards the bear.

He pushed off with his right hand and knees, then dug in with his boots and dove directly over Lucky. The bear's massive head was snaking downward towards Lucky as Buck fell under its open jaws.

Buck landed on his side, lying on top of Lucky's prone form. His .44 was clutched in his left hand. He was completely covered by the bear, pressed down by its bulk. The bear's fur stunk of decayed and dying flesh and the rank sour smell of the wild. Pushing the barrel of the gun into the tangled fur, he pulled the trigger of the .44 over and over, feeling with each percussion the gun jumping in his hand, each shot exploding right next to his face, pounding his ears while his eyes and hands were lost in the matted wet hair.

The bear twisted above him and Buck felt a sharp pain in his head followed by the hot warmth of blood running down the side of his face. He could hear a tearing sound and it took a second before he realized his scalp was being pulled from his head. He felt his body being jerked upward and was shocked at the incredible strength he felt in the bear's jaws. Suddenly he was released. The bear moved away from him and he fell to the ground next to Lucky who struggled to push Buck aside and get up. The white snow was marked with red and dark with dirt and leaves where they had struggled.

Buck lay on his side, his .44 still in his hand, watching the bear with eyes blurred and out of focus. The bear stood swaying on all fours, silently watching them from several steps away, then it turned, grunting and fiercely shaking its head, scattering bright red blood over the snow. Finally, it disappeared into the trees and brush, heading down the mountain.

Buck struggled to his knees and tried to help Lucky up. Turning, he could see Sister Toni pushing herself out of the snow and Jesse still huddled up against the granite.

Sister Toni awkwardly stood then brushed the snow off her cloak, holding out her arm and gingerly testing its motion. She appeared near spent, beaten down by Mac's course and the violence of the attack. Then looking more closely at Buck, she stopped, realizing that Buck was bleeding.

She called out, "Oh God, he's hurt, Buck's hurt, Jesse, come help." Then she knelt down beside Buck and reached for his torn head.

"Oh Buck, you fool, you brave, crazy fool."

Buck knelt in the snow, grinning and swaying like he was drunk, blood still dripping from his head, a chunk of hair and skin pulled back, out of place.

"You're the crazy one," he answered.

And suddenly Lucky was next to Buck, pounding him on the back, shouting, "Goddamn Buck, you tackled that bastard and gave him a belly full, I thought I was a goner." Lucky whooped, grabbed Jesse as she stood up and squeezed her then fell to his knees and hugged Buck with both arms.

"You're a fuckin' warrior man."

Abruptly Lucky quit celebrating. "Oh shit," he exclaimed. Buck had turned on his knees and was slowly sliding to the ground, still smiling his goofy grin, the .44 slipping from his grasp. Toni and Lucky gently laid him on his back, his head resting in Toni's lap.

When Buck woke, it was dark, his head throbbed and he was thirsty. He looked up into the eyes of Sister Toni.

"What about Mac? Is Mac okay?"

Lucky knelt beside him. "Mac's on his own for now. We talked it over while you were out. It's dark and the bear may still be out there, madder than hell." Looking at Buck's head, the wound now clotted with dried blood and a salve Toni applied, he continued, "We can't be splittin' up right now."

Lucky shook his head, grimacing darkly, "I wanted to go, go try to catch 'em and stop him, that dumb asshole, but it jus' can't be done right now. He would've agreed, I think, if he were makin' the call."

Lucky stood and glanced at Toni, "We've got to care for each other now. Mac 'il do what he does." Sister Toni lifted Buck's head up and wrapped the wound and salve with gauze, then laid Buck's head back onto the hood of his coat. She looked up at Lucky, nodding in agreement. Buck started to protest, trying to sit up, saying that he was okay, that they should go and leave him, but Sister Toni gently pulled him back.

"Buck, whatever Mac was planning was likely done and over long before that damn bear attacked anyway. There's nothing we can do now to change things." Buck could see the tears in Toni's eyes as she turned and wiped her face with her sleeve. "So we will get some sleep and then we'll take stock and decide what to do. Right now I don't know, I just don't know." As Buck fell back asleep, his head resting in Sister Toni's lap, the last thing he saw in the firelight were her lonely haunted eyes staring into the dark.

Away from the fire, Lucky and Jesse sat, huddled together. "Do you think he'll be alright?" Jesse asked, sitting up, wrapped in a blanket.

"Sister knows a bit about medicine. If he's not feverish he'll be okay. We can find a doctor when we get down anyways."

They both were quiet, both watching the darkness, wondering about the bear. Finally, Jesse broke the silence.

"So how'd you get hooked up with Mac?"

Lucky looked down at the slight slender form huddled next to him. Putting his arm around her, warming her against the night, he could feel the narrowness of her shoulders, small and fragile in his grasp. He felt a desire to talk to her. To tell her about himself and Mac, to push back his fear for Mac's safety.

"Well, we, my mom and me, we always figured that Mac might be my Dad. At least that's what my Mom tol' me 'fore she died. I'd hear stories 'bout him when I was a kid, people said things, jest talkin' you know. Mac was famous in these parts, kind of a hero and scary at the same time, but I'd never seen him, not face to face." Lucky was quiet for a time and then continued, "My Mom died when I was eleven. My Mom's half-brother had a logging operation up near the border and after my Mom passed he and his wife came to our house, cleaning it out I guess, getting ready to haul my ass out to somewhere. I didn't know him or his wife and sure didn't like 'em much. Didn't have any other relatives that I liked any better though, so I didn't think I had much of a choice in the matter."

Lucky felt Jesse scooting closer and he tightened his grip on her shoulders and then continued to talk.

"Anyways, I was standin' in the kitchen and screaming at my aunt who was shakin' me and tryin' to explain the way things were, when the door was kicked open and this crazy looking guy is standing there. He just looked at me for a while and then he turned to my aunt and said, 'My son's comin' with me,' and he pointed out the door with his lips the way he does. Well, I grabbed my stuff and ran out of the door to an ol' truck he had parked outside and hopped in." Lucky paused, reflecting, "Beat the hell out of the alternative as Mac would say."

"I could hear my uncle and aunt sputtering and gabbing at Mac 'bout their rights and all, but Mac he just walked right passed them folks and ran 'cross the yard and jumped into the truck beside me. We hauled ass out of there with them runnin' after us and yellin' as we pulled away. I remember I asked him three things. First I asked him, 'Are you my Dad?' and he said, 'Well kid, I don't rightly know but we'll play it that way for now if that's okay with you.' And I nodded and hung onto the door as we slid around the corner. Next I asked, since I'd watched enough TV to know that they just needed the license plate to find him, 'Can't they just trace the truck?' and he just looked at me and grinned, 'Stole it!' he responded, raising his eyebrows. Finally I asked, 'Where we goin?' and he said, 'To the mountains kid, to the mountains.' He's been my Dad ever since and now the dumb fuck's gone off to have ol' McLaren shoot him. Jesus!"

Jesse stayed close, holding on to Lucky. "I hope your Dad is okay, I liked him." She pulled the blanket tighter around her shoulders. "You know I think he's sweet on Sister Toni. She's powerful lonely at times." They sat in silence for a while longer then Jesse spoke again. "I had a step-dad for a while, more of a foster dad, after my mom left." She stopped, her head now resting against Lucky's chest. "He hurt me," she confided in a quiet voice. Lucky looked down at her, thinking of the cold and the bear and said to her, "Not sure it's gotten much better, this cock up."

"Its better," Jesse responded, carefully watching the darkness around the fire.

The night deepened and the cold started once again to reach deep into Toni's joints. She sat holding Buck's head and tried to rid herself of an undefined panic that kept creeping into her mind, pushing back her faith and hope and filling her with despair. She kept thinking that Mac might be dead. Her breath caught once and then she deliberately took another deep breath and tried to talk to God but she couldn't. She just couldn't bring herself to form the words. She didn't think she could face going back, back to hauling water and birthin' lambs and shouldering the burden of all those lost souls needing care without Mac nearby.

CHAPTER EIGHT

Now I am fled
My soul is in the sky
Tongue, lose thy light
Moon, take thy flight
Now, die, die, die, die. 8

Late in the night Buck lay with his head in Sister Toni's lap. His eyes were closed against the hurt, drawing in the warmth of Toni's thighs that were pressed against the side of his face. He tried to contain the pain that was throbbing from somewhere deep inside, a pain that would occasionally and without warning flare up, shooting across his eyes and scalp. When that happened he would grimace in response, rising a bit from Toni's lap, his face and eyes taut. At those times, Sister Toni's soothing hand would lightly caress the skin around his wounds and she would pull the heavy canvas sleeping bag back over his shoulders and murmur words of comfort.

The ground beneath him was strong and unyielding. He could feel the coldness of the mountain but was warm in his bedding. He thought about the pain then tried not to think about the pain and finally, helplessly, he just let it move through him, steeling himself against its ebb and flow, taking comfort in Toni's gentle hands.

Buck thought about times long past when he'd been in pain and held in other arms. Unlike this moment, where he was soothed by Toni's caress, he could not recall taking much comfort in those past gestures. Usually, when he was afraid or hurting he felt only a need to push away, to seek protection in movement, to be alone. Somewhere in the past, he had learned that if he closed off all paths of contact, he could make the pain go away.

Buck also could remember late nights when he would lay awake in bed and be overcome by an un-defined sense of fear and foreboding. It would slide past all his defenses and make his heart race, leaving him covered with sweat and twisted in his sheets. When that happened he would bury his face in his arms, clamp shut his eyes and wait.

Wait for the big bad feeling to go away.

As he got older, Buck had learned ways to keep these fears at bay. Each troubled morning or worrisome evening he would conjure up dreams and fantasies of what he would or could do, rebuilding in his mind a series of events that provided some peace and contentment, slowly constructing what, he saw now, was just a lifelong process of retreat. He would live in the artificial world that he had so carefully constructed, missing most of what actually occurred.

Just like Mac, he was losing pieces of himself, often without even knowing the pieces were gone.

Now, lying on the side of the mountain, Buck realized that none of those efforts really worked. Any illusion of comfort that he constructed was often marred by a small worry or persistent thought that he couldn't push away, leaving him in a state of anxiety that always diminished whatever pleasure he hoped to enjoy.

Buck saw his past with a newfound clarity. He understood Mac's disdain for his meager justifications. He realized that he had quit trying to truly be alive a long time ago. Instead, he had embraced a state of being that was comfortable but careful, tentative. He had followed a path that increasingly lacked in content and required little courage.

As he lay now in Toni's lap, he took some solace in his pain and the memory of the violent force of the bear's jaws. At least it was real. At least now he felt that he was a part of the substance of the life that surrounded him. For the moment, he felt no compulsion to distance himself. He let the present soak into him like water satisfying a long and unquenched thirst.

Turning his head, he raised his hand from the canvas bag and grasped the thin and chilled fingers that caressed his forehead. He opened his eyes to look directly into Sister Toni's.

"Is your God here, Sister?"

Toni, her hand in his, next to his cheek, squeezed gently.

"Don't you feel his strength?"

"I feel strength, Sister, but I think it may be coming from you or maybe just from myself."

"I wouldn't worry too much about the source Buck."

"Have you figured out what God has in mind for us this time, Sister? Why we're here, the bear, Mac leaving, you figured any of that out?

"No, I don't have any answers for that, Buck, no answers at all."

She shifted her warmth beneath his head and lifted her hand from his, once more pulling the canvas bag tightly around his shoulders. Then placing her hand back on his chest, she said, "Now rest, morning is coming soon." Buck closed his eyes and thought of Mac and being on the mountain without him and then he thought of his wife and her hands as they had rested on his shoulders, and then he slept.

◆ ◆ ◆ ◆

Near midday, Mac had almost completed his circular path around the mountain, nearing its north face, just below the tree line. The snow continued to fall as he moved from faint deer paths to old logging roads and back, staying clear of the thick brush and keeping just beneath the granite slabs strewn across the upper slope of the mountain. At one point he approached a section of the forest where thousands of limbs and small trees were piled up, leaning in every direction and blocking his passage, forcing him for a time down into the brush and the berries. Finally he came across a forest service trail that he knew wound its way down from the summit, and he followed the zigzag trail from the side of the mountain towards the rambling log home of Moses McLaren.

The closer Mac came to McLaren's home the less excited he was about his plan. He slowed his pace and began to consider the alternatives. For a time the best option he could come up with was to find his'self some tequila and curl up next to a fire to wait out the snow and his new found sense of responsibility.

But then he smelled the smoke from a wood stove and walking even more slowly, he crept around a twist in the trail and spied McLaren's cabin tucked deep into the side of a ravine. The ramshackle structure was hunkered down beneath a stand of old growth cedar, massive trunks towering over the rough-hewn wood and hand split shakes. To the right side of the house was a boulder standing as high as the roof, covered with yellow and green. Mac stood quietly and watched the snow slowly filter down through the trees, white against the forest green needles, dipped with frost.

The scent of burning wood awakened memories of campfires past and older times, easier times. He recalled when he and Lucky would sit around a fire and talk about folks and the woods, the air touched with the taste of smoke and the scent of damp clothes and cold boots warmed by the heat of the flames. They would sip whiskey and make plans, big plans that Moses seemed bent on disrupting, one way or another.

Mac knew that McLaren lived the old way. He followed the code and the code required vengeance. To him, shooting Lucky was a near reflex action or instinct necessitated by his own son's killin'. McLaren was past thoughts of compassion or consequences or even hell's fire. He had long ago reconciled himself to that end and didn't much seem to care. If Mac walked away now, he knew it would only be a matter of time before McLaren would hunt Lucky down. In his burdened mind there were no other paths that he could take. But Mac figured he had an ace, a lever to put an end to that string of vengeance and to keep Lucky alive. If it cost him, well, he certainly didn't deserve any extra days, not with all he had walked away from, all the needed things he just hadn't done.

The snow was swirling in the rising wind and thickening, obscuring the colors of the hillside, suffusing the cedar stand with a soft and dimming light. As Mac continued to quietly stand before the cabin, he recalled the last time he had seen McLaren, years before. He had come upon McLaren's truck parked at an angle along the side of the access road leading to this cabin. The back end of the truck was jutting out into the rutted lane of travel. Mac had walked out of the trees and walked towards the open driver's door and saw McLaren laid out over his steering wheel, his body racked with silent spasms. When Mac approached, McLaren slowly turned and looked at him. His voice was horse and barely more than a whisper.

"I don' killed that little girl, Mac, I let Anna go off by herself and get hurt by those men and goddamn druggies and didn't do a thing." His voice had strengthened then, and he had looked at Mac with the old fervor that Mac remembered from his youth.

"My own flesh and my own blood, chased away by my pride. That little baby was hurt and hurt again while I sat up here and chewed on my righteous thinking and didn't do nothin!" His empty eyes then looked right through Mac, at something in the past, something he couldn't face, not then. McLaren cranked the engine, and it had caught and he pulled away, the driver's door swinging until McLaren reached out and yanked it shut. Mac knew he was going home to his son, Ian, to all he had left.

Mac didn't go after him, just walked down the road in the other direction, his own mind filled with the memory of an evening in Butte, a few years earlier, when he'd also let Anna down. That particular night he'd been cruising the town, seeing friends, drinking whiskey, tearing up a bit. When he came out of a favorite watering hole, he almost ran into a little girl wrapped in an oversized jacket. It was Anna. She stood before him, skinny, shaking, her eyes tearing up, and she had begged him.

"Just a little money, Mac, just this one time, just something to help me git set up."

He remembered the raw fear in her eyes as she had cried for help. But Mac had looked away and without saying a word, turned and walked down the sidewalk. He left her on the street, not even looking back. He'd been too damn afraid to get tied up with Anna's messed up life, didn't want the bother, and he'd kept on walking until he had found a stool at an unfamiliar bar and sat and drank and tried to forget the look on her face.

Now, standing in the snow and silence, he remembered a time even further back, when he was a dumb little kid, short and fat and just starting to harden up underneath. He and Anna had spent one of those magic summers kids could have when they didn't know any better, a summer just pal'in around. A summer sliding on their backsides, slick as otters, down the icy rapids of the river, screaming and hooting then fishing in the early morning with broomsticks and nylon that Mac had stole from the mercantile.

Standing there in the snow and silence outside McLaren's home, Mac remembered warm summer evenings sitting on an old canvas bag in front of a campfire way out in the woods. He and Anna had sat together, huddled against the dark and scary, spellbound by Moses McLaren standing tall and dark, backlit by the dancing flames of the fire, waving his arms and telling them all about Jill and Bill and their Dad Bill Bungle who lived way up in the hills, way up in these old hills, way up in the hills that were Mac's home.

Mac pulled off his hat and knocked off the snow, brushing it from his coat, then yanked his hat down tight. He rubbed his face with both hands, feeling the sting of the cold and the heat of his hands and then the creeping numbness in his feet. No, he thought, his plan was the right way to go. He'd walked away too many times and hid from his guilt behind so many bottles that he didn't have much right to even call himself a man. No, this was right, here right now, this was right. Mac stamped his frozen feet then strode out into the clearing in front of the cabin and called out, "McLaren you old son-of-a-bitch I've got business with you!"

McLaren sat as he often did, in his old rocker on the deck, his rifle in his lap, a bottle, half empty, set down next to the chair. He sat facing the clearing with his mind empty, the shape of his thoughts forged by the hopeless years long gone by. He looked up when he heard Mac and when he registered the challenge in Mac's voice he just felt tired. He wondered if the kid was here too, so he could just finish it, fulfill his obligation, and quietly slip away.

Mac came within fifty feet or so and stopped, hands out and legs spread.

"I'm not armed Moses. We got a few things we need to discuss."

"It's no use talking to me about the boy. He kilt mine and has to pay with his' own. That's the way it is." He raised the barrel of his rifle in Mac's direction as he spoke.

"I'm here to offer a trade," Mac responded quietly, just loud enough for McLaren to hear.

"You got nothin' and I'm not interested." McLaren reached down for his bottle, his eyes never leaving Mac.

"My life, you stupid bastard, my life's gotta' be worth something. You shoot me and give me your word you'll leave my boy alone. That's what I got."

McLaren just looked at him and took a pull on the bottle.

"You want me to kill you 'stead of your boy?" McLaren slowly raised himself up holding the gun in one hand and the bottle in the other. "You think you're some kind of goddamned savior now?" McLaren was silent for a moment then continued quietly. "That don't seem to revenge my boy all too well Mac."

"I got something else." Mac swallowed. "I can give you something to live for, McLaren. Give you something back for Anna." Mac stopped talking and looked down at the ground. "Give you something back for me not helping Anna, I didn't, you know, didn't help her when she asked, there in the end. I just walked away."

"What the hell do you think you can give me?" McLaren shouted, dropping his bottle to the deck and grabbing the rifle in two hands. "What do you think you are promising me? Don't you dare be bringin' my little girl into this. I'll shoot you and that kid, I will."

McLaren's voice was hoarse with the whiskey and the emotion, his eyes fearful, questioning. He was silent for a moment then looked at Mac and finished, quietly. "What can you give me?"

"Her daughter, your granddaughter, McLaren," Mac called out. "She's alive, she's a young woman. She's not fair like Anna. She's got dark fierce eyes, eyes just like yours. I can give you that if you give me your word. I'll tell you where she is and then you can shoot me and be done with it."

Mac stood there, chest out, waiting. He'd played his last card, had nothing left. McLaren looked down at him and raised his rifle, aiming straight at Mac.

"You got my word."

And then Mac told him, told him where they were and what he knew and then he stopped, feeling the cool air on his face, smelling the sharp scent of the cedars now wet with snow and watching the ice crystals sparkling as the sun broke through. McLaren, his gun tucked into his shoulder, looked at Mac for a moment and then muttered, "I'm sorry Mac," and pulled the trigger.

CHAPTER NINE

He goes before me and still dares me on
When I come where he calls, then he is gone. 9

Sister Toni had fallen asleep, slumped over Buck, when she was awakened by Lucky's hand on her shoulder. It was still night and above her, mid the stars and constellations, the silver crescent of a new moon gleamed.

"Sister, you awake?" Lucky whispered.

Toni nodded, looking up at the sky then at Lucky.

"Me and Jesse have been talking. I'm thinkin' we should be getting off of this mountain now, before morning when the sun starts meltin' the snow. These rocks are goin' to be awful slick." He paused, looking back at Jesse.

"And sister, I'm still worried about Mac. I know we're probably too late to matter, but we're just a half hour or so from the summit where there's a forest service trail. Sister, that trail runs right down to McLaren's if you follow it far enough. I know we couldn't up and leave before with Buck bleeding all over but, well, if he can walk, it's got to be better off the mountain than stuck up here." Lucky stood up, not whispering anymore, "I think we should head to that trail. If Buck can move, we should go."

Sister Toni looked around their camp. She could tell it was close to morning. She felt Buck's head, his wounds had bound and weren't bleeding. What had seemed confusing to her last night seemed a lot clearer now. Lucky was right, it was time to move, and if going to the top was the way to go, well that felt right too.

She nodded, "Okay, we'll go." She gently shook Buck until his eyes opened.

He smiled then grimaced, closing his eyes, mumbling, "Hurts, just sleep, just a little longer."

Toni, ignoring him, put her hand behind his neck. "Let's try to sit up now, nice and easy." She helped Buck to a sitting position then spoke quietly. "Buck, Lucky thinks we need to go now and find the forest service trail that heads down to McLaren's. I agree. Do you think you can walk?" More fully awake now, Buck slowly nodded then reached out his hand and Lucky and Toni helped him to his feet. He stood for a moment, gingerly moving his head.

"I can walk."

Buck sat down, already breaking out in a sweat from the effort of standing, while Lucky, Toni and Jesse pulled camp and packed Bob-a-Lou and themselves. Handing Buck her walking stick, Toni stood and looked over everyone then said, "Okay let's go. The sun will be up soon." They followed Lucky up a steep incline of bear grass and rocks. The trees and slope appeared as shadows, the details of the ground before them difficult to see. They carefully stepped where the person in front of them stepped, watching the light from Lucky's flashlight dance and jerk over the snow and trees. At the top of the ridge the trees disappeared except for a few lonely alpine fir and large blocks of granite as big as cars that were scattered haphazardly, the edges of the stones softened by the night and the thin cover of snow. After hiking for a half hour they stopped. A rock field lay before them, a dark jumble of shadows that contrasted with the slowly lightening sky.

Jesse had spent the last half hour following in the footsteps of Lucky, comfortable in his shadow, her mind whirling with thoughts of him and the bear and the dark majesty of the massive stones they passed. As she circled those stones she would let her hand drag lightly against the smooth cold surface, letting her imagination touch the echoes of ancient times that seemed to be calling to her, comforting her. She found herself smiling, sharing a quiet secret with the mountain as she slipped on the uneven ground, balancing on the thin edges of the upright stones and slowly progressing against the pitch into the thinning dawn air.

They were all breathing hard when they stopped, their breath visible in the cold air as they stood heavy on their feet, looking up at the steep rock field leading to the top of the mountain.

Lucky pointed to a spot near the edge of the summit. "The trail from the other side comes to the top, right there on the left."

They could see no way to cross the rocks ahead without climbing each slab and dropping to the next. Many of the pieces were resting at a near vertical angle. Sister Toni folded her gloved hands before her for a moment, bowed her head and then looked up at the others. "I think we should wait, just for a minute." She turned and helped Buck sit down and held her canteen to his lips. "How are you holding up Buck?" Buck, his hand shaking, covered her hand with his on the canteen and drank, then said, "Okay." He lowered the canteen but still held his hand over Toni's. His hands were hot and damp. "I've been worrying about Mac."

Releasing her hand, he looked into her eyes.

"I've never met a man who chased death so hard. I've been down that road myself but I would just curl up into a ball with drink or whatever and wait it out. Mac seems to get more alive the worse it gets, and now he's gone and done this. I just don't get it. Can't figure him out."

Sister Toni took a deep breath.

"I know. I'm afraid I..."

Toni was cut short when Lucky shouted.

"Son of a bitch!"

Toni turned, and standing fifty yards away, its head up and weaving back and forth, was the bear. Lucky was raising his rifle to shoot just as the sun slipped over the mountains to the east, momentarily blinding him. He reached up and pulled down the rim of his hat trying to get a clean line when Jesse called out, pulling on his coat.

"Lucky, Lucky look! Look at the mountain!" They all turned and saw the sun touching the rock field. A few feet from where they stood a clear path was apparent between two rocks that they thought had been one. It was a narrow crevice, but wide enough to squeeze through. Toni yelled, "Go! Go! Run!" And she pushed Buck up towards the crevice. Bob-a-Lou brayed and ran to the right, away from the bear. Toni ran up the slope, forcing Buck into the narrow opening ahead of her with Jesse right on her heels. Lucky was walking backwards facing the bear, still trying to get a shot when the bear roared and charged, and he turned and ran.

Buck pulled himself through the crack in the rock, trying to keep ahead of the panicked group behind him. On both sides the rock field quickly rose above his head and he could see the narrow slit of sky above turning light blue with dawn. He felt Toni's hands on his back, pushing up behind him as he struggled up the uneven slope.

Lucky hit the fissure just before the bear but still couldn't get off a shot. The sun was now full over the eastern horizon and hit him right in the eyes. As he crawled through the rocks he reached out and jammed the stock of his gun into a vertical crack he saw in the uphill stone and, heart pumping at the sight of the bear, now a dark charging shadow surrounded by the brilliant light of the new sun, pulled down as hard as he could on the gun stock and dislodged the granite wedge. The rock fell across the opening just before the point where it narrowed. The bear hit the fallen rock just inches from Lucky as he scrambled back, finally able to fire his rifle. He could see the bear's face, its eye mangled, black blood clotted on its neck. Lucky fired a final time then turned and ran up the path behind Jesse. The bear, still alive and raging, was stopped by the rocks in its path. It rammed itself repeatedly against the smaller stone, roaring with each assault, trying to dislodge the rock but succeeded only in jamming it more firmly into the breech. By the time Lucky had caught up with Jesse and Toni, the bear had fallen silent. The three of them stood, listening for a minute, and then they could hear the bear shuffling away from the opening, rocks rattling and falling as it moved down the slope away from them. The three of them leaned on one another, hugging, reassuring themselves that they were safe, then looked up the path and saw Buck disappearing ahead and pushed upward to follow.

Buck came out of the narrow path onto a knoll of grass, damp with melting snow, and fell to his knees. Breathing deeply, he felt his head pounding where his scalp had been injured and it was a minute before he realized what was before him. As Toni, Jesse and Lucky stumbled out of the fissure behind him he looked out at a small valley that sloped gently downward and was surrounded by steep cliffs. The valley ended in a small canyon, thick with trees. The west wall was lit by sunshine and to the right the sun cut rainbows through a cloud of dense steam rising from a pool of water. Son of a bitch, he thought to himself, this is Jesse's valley, the magic valley. Looking up he saw a stream of water pouring clean and clear from the side of the cliff into the pool.

The others stopped and were staring with wonder as the rising sun slowly filled the valley, the snow was melting and running in shimmering sheets of water that danced and sparkled as they fell down the black and gray walls, disappearing under the early snow on the floor of the valley.

Jesse pushed past Lucky and Buck, slowly walking towards the water streaming from the side of the rock. Hesitantly she reached out and placed first her fingers, then her hand into the stream. She cupped her hands, filling them with the water then bent over and drank deeply, water and tears running down her cheeks, her voice choked by emotion.

She cried, "Oh, Sister, it is real." And the memories of her mother, holding her as a small child in her lap and looking at her with eyes sparkling and alive, returned to her. Memories clean and clear, the love in her mother's face warm and real. Jesse turned and lay her damp check against Lucky's rough beard.

"I can feel her Lucky, I can touch her." Sobbing, she held Lucky as Buck and Toni both approached the water and drank, and then Jesse grabbed Lucky's hat off his head, filled it, and brought it to Lucky's mouth.

Their reverence was broken by a single shot, its echo ricocheting back and forth across the valley. Lucky looked up towards the cliffs, thinking he recognized the sound of that rifle, looking apprehensively at Buck then quickly looking back at the cliffs as three more shots rang out in quick succession followed by two more. Lucky suddenly threw his hat in

the air and whooped and started running back towards the entrance of the valley just as Mac's rotund
figure squeezed sideways out of the fissure. He was
muttering, pulling his coat and hat back in place,
just in time to be hit full force by Lucky, who
knocked him ass over teakettle. Both of them
laughed and rolled on the ground. Mac shouted,
"Jesus Christ, you idiot," then roughly rubbed his
fist over Lucky's bare head and heaved himself up.

When he got to his feet, he found himself standing directly in front of Sister Toni. They both were
silent for a momen,t and then Mac opened his arms
and Toni walked quickly into his embrace.

"Oh Mac," Toni murmured, holding tight, eyes
closed, coursed through with love. Mac looked over
Toni's shoulder at Buck and grinned, "Found your
mule, boyo." Buck just shook his head.

For a moment, no one noticed the tall figure
that slipped out of the rock, his long rifle resting
comfortably in his hand. Then Lucky looked up but
before he could rise felt Mac's strong hand holding
him down.

"It's alright son." He patted Lucky's shoulder,
and loosening his hold on Toni, cleared his throat and
addressed the group.

"Folks, I'd like to introduce those who don't
know him to Moses McLaren. Now," holding his
hands up to forestall any questions, "Now I know

you're aware me and McLaren have had our differences." He looked at McLaren who just nodded, stone-faced. "But we've been interacting some and other than this little hole in my hat," he said, fingering a hole in the top of his oilskin, "nothin's goin' to come of it."

Mac look at McLaren who started to speak, then stopped. Looking over at Lucky he finally said, "We're square."

Mac then walked over to Jesse and held one of her hands in both of his. "Jesse, I want to introduce you to someone." And he walked Jesse, who had a puzzled look but a smile dancing on her lips, over to stand before McLaren. Mac then formally made his introduction.

"I want you to meet your granddad, your mother's pa."

CHAPTER 10

Follow me then to plainer ground. 10

Buck sat on the edge of the porch of the Lightning Strike Tavern. The morning was warm, an Indian summer. The snow was gone, at least for a time. The tavern sat all alone at the end of a dirt road two or three miles from the highway. It was quiet. Muted voices and the sound of glasses clinking could be heard from inside. As his face soaked in the sun, he fingered the stitches the doctor had put in his head and smiled with the memory of Lucky's account of the bear fight. If Lucky kept talking and gilding the lily like he'd been doing Buck would be the next Davy Crockett in this valley. The folks at the tavern already looked at him with a respect that he thought was both a little funny and felt good.

Earlier, McLaren had brought over his truck and trailer, handed him the keys and mumbled,

"Fixed the cab light and radio for ye." Then looking up at Buck, he grabbed his hand.

"Thanks for watching out for my little girl Buck."

Buck just nodded, thinking of Sister Toni's reckless charge, wondering who the real heroes were. McLaren had turned to leave when Buck stopped him with a hand on his shoulder.

"Hold on just a sec."

He reached into the cab and removed the LC Smith from its rack and placed it in McLaren's hands.

"This has been sitting on a lot of mantles over the years. It's a beautiful piece. Time it came off the wall. I'd like you to have it, they say it shoots true."

They both were quiet for a moment then Buck added, "It's good to have Mac here."

McLaren stood before him, his hands gently holding the shotgun, turning it a bit one way and the other, taking in its weight and feel.

"I'll take good care of it," he said, then nodded once and walked away.

Sitting back on the steps, Buck thought about the look of quiet surprise on McLaren's face when he'd handed him the gun, then his brief smile when he mentioned Mac. Buck's past and McLaren's and Mac and this valley all touched in one way or another. The shotgun was fair payment Buck thought, tied all of them together somehow. He wondered about McLaren's fate and Mac's and what was next for him. He sat in the sun feeling warm and rested, well grounded in the here and now, waiting for his wife.

When he had called her, all he could think of was holding her and her touch and the sound of her voice. The distance that he had imagined before the trip just wasn't there. It was as if the joy in her voice had reappeared. More likely, he thought, he'd just been unable or unwilling to hear it. As he breathed in the clean air, tasting it, gently rubbing his head, he wondered what else he'd missed.

Buck heard the car before he saw the cloud of dust drifting towards him from the valley floor.

Buck stood, slowly walking down the steps as their chevy wagon pulled into the yard and stopped. Melinda opened the door and jumped out, running to him, carefully holding him, looking into his face and eyes and lightly tracing his scars. "Jesus Buck what have you done with yourself?" Buck just closed his eyes and hugged her back and they stood in the sun until they heard someone clearing their throat up on the porch.

Buck looked around and letting Melinda go for a moment took her hand and said, "I'd like you to meet a good friend of mine. I gotta' caution you, he's a bit on the crazy side."

Mac, hat in hand, walked down the steps and nodded tentatively to Melinda. He tipped his head a bit as he looked at her then grabbed her hand and pulled her into a bear hug.

Stepping back he said, "It's my honor to meet ya ma'am." Still holding her at arm's length, he turned to Buck and said, "This is one fine piece of woman you got here, boyo." Then he leaned forward and kissed Melinda gently on the cheek. "We're pretty partial to your Buck here."

Smiling, he reached into his pocket and pulled out his flask. "A little medicine?" he asked, raising his bushy eyebrows and holding out the bottle. Buck shook his head, he'd had more than enough of Mac's medicine lately and was surprised when Melinda took the flask and upended it for a full swallow, grimacing before she exhaled loudly and wiped her mouth. She handing the flask back to Mac.

"You gotta' buy some better booze, mister."

Then holding on to Buck's arm, she asked, "You got any more characters I need to meet?" Buck put his hand over hers and they walked up the steps. Mac held the door open for them as they walked inside.

◆ ◆ ◆ ◆

The late fall night came early, even before the chores were completed. Sister Toni was sitting on her bench watching the evening settle in. She'd talked to

God a lot lately and felt a great comfort from the conversations. It had taken a while to bring things to a conclusion but she knew now that it was time to finally end the loneliness she had been living with.

Mac was out in the hills somewhere tonight. Said he'd buy her breakfast at the Lightning and she smiled, thinking it had been a lot of years since a man offered to buy her breakfast. As she sat rocking in the cold, bundled in the soft wool blanket she had made with her own hands, she listened to Lucky and Jesse inside laughing. Oh my God, she thought, who would have ever imagined old man McLaren laughing with those two youngsters in my kitchen. The only word McLaren would say about his and Mac's encounter was that he'd missed. Short and simple. Toni shook her head, a very strange and complicated man, now all of a sudden full of a tentative kind of joy. If she didn't know better she'd think that the water on the mountain was magic.

Toni thought about Jesse's story and where its seed had been planted and by whom and decided to just let it go. Sitting and rocking warm in the cold, she rested, her feet drawn up under the blanket. Maybe she'd just fall asleep out here tonight, surrounded by the mountains, by Mac's mountains, watching over her.

◆ ◆ ◆

The next day Buck and Mac sat on the back of the opened horse trailer, waiting for Melinda and Toni to come back from the cabin they were cleaning up for Jesse. "So Mac," Buck asked, "What are your plans?"

Mac sighed, "We're charting new waters here Bucko. I guess I'm going to inch along for a while. I thought about doing a little prospectin'. Toni," he coughed then cleared his throat, "Toni says that might be a constructive use of my wanderlust as she calls it." They both were quiet for a moment.

"I've got something for you." Mac reached into his pocket and pulled out an object wrapped in a fold of soft leather then stood and faced Buck.

"You know, courage is a funny thing. You think it's a part of you, a piece of who you are and then when you need it, it might just be missin'. Sometimes a man needs a little help remembrin' the times when he stands up and is counted." Mac looked at Buck then folded back the leather and lying in the fold was a large bear claw, a small hole drilled at the thick end, looped through with a leather strap.

"It's your bear son. McLaren finally put him down, mean ol' fucker." Mac lifted up the rawhide string and placed it over Buck's head as Buck struggled to his feet. Then Mac took Buck's face in his hands and kissed him right on the mouth. Pulling back, he smiled and squeezed Buck's shoulders. A noise to their left caused them both to turn. Toni, Melinda, Jesse and Lucky were all standing quietly next to the truck. Melinda was wiping a tear from her eye with her sleeve and then Lucky broke the spell by walking forward and hugging Buck. "Don't be a stranger."

Buck nodded and started to clear a spot in the trailer for the donkey when Mac scooted off around the side of the rig and came back leading Bob-a-Lou. He reached into the trailer and grabbed the blanket and packs, throwing them on Bob-a-Lou's back and bent over, tightening the cinch. Then he stood up and looked at Buck. "I'm thinking," he started, raising his eyebrows, "I'm thinking that this old mule'd be better off with me for a while, with my prospectin' plans and all."

Mac stood there in the afternoon sun, his head back and his barrel chest thrown out, daring Buck with a challenge in his eye. Buck just looked at him for a minute and shook his head. Then he turned away and closed the back door of the trailer before he unhooked the trailer from the truck.

"It's a loan old man."

"You betcha, boyo."

Mac spun on his boots, gave Bob-a-Lou a jerk, and started walking towards the forest. "Sister, you up for a long soak in a hot springs I recently discovered?"

Toni just smiled and walked with him, touching Buck once, lightly on the shoulder, as she passed.

Waving at Lucky and hugging Jesse, Buck turned and looked at Melinda, "The chevy?"

"We'll pick it up later, I'm riding with you on this trip."

Buck opened the truck door and crawled in, reaching across and unlocking the door for Melinda. As they started down the dirt road they could see Toni and Mac just entering the cover of the trees, Mac's hands were waving around and Toni was looking up at him.

With his arm resting on the windowsill and his wife at his side, Buck drove down the twisting gravel road, driving away from the mountain.

Melinda looked over at Buck, started to say something then thought better of it. After a moment, she turned again to Buck.

"Stop the truck."

Buck looked over at her, a question on his face, then nodded and pulled off the road. When the truck had stopped she reached up and caught the back of Buck's head with her hand then leaned forward and kissed Buck on the lips, hard then softer, his mouth opening to hers. Then she leaned back and looked directly into his eyes.

"Welcome home, boyo."

NOTES

1. *A Midsummer Night's Dream*, Act 1, Scene 1, lines 8-10; the palace of Theseus. Hippolyta is speaking to Theseus and others of their wedding, which is to occur in four days under a new moon. In the play and in *Mountain Lyrics*, the words mark the beginning of a passage from order to uncertainty, then back again to circumstances that may appear to be the same but have been irrevocably changed.

2. *A Midsummer Night's Dream*, Act 2, Scene 2, line 150; a wood near Athens. Oberon, the king of the fairies, is speaking to Puck, his jester, and Titania, his wife, the queen of the fairies. At the outset, their love is beset with difficulties, out of balance. In these verses, Oberon recalls the powerful call of the "sea maid's music" and it is followed by verses discussing cupid's loosed arrow that misses its mark. It seemed an appropriate introduction to Sister Toni's star-shrouded valley, her attraction to Mac and the tension between that attraction and her chosen life style.

3. *A Midsummer Night's Dream*, Act 2, scene 1, line 5; again in the woods near Athens. The fairy in these verses, Titania's attendant, speaks these words in response to Puck's query, "How now, spirit! Whither wander you?" Mac and Buck's journey into the wilderness started in just the same way. "Over hill, over dale." Mac also has a bit of the mischievous nature of Puck, a fellow "merry wanderer of the night," (2.1.43). Finally, the unpredictable twinnings of fate that soon beset Mac, Buck and all their company reflect themes found in Titania's speech to Oberon (2.1.81-117), where "the spring, the summer, the childing autumn, angry winter, change their wonted liveries; and the mazed world, by their increase, now knows not which is which."

4. *A Midsummer Night's Dream*, Act 3, scene 1, lines 78-79; Puck is speaking of a group of craftsman, including Bottom, the overconfident weaver, who have congregated in the woods to rehearse a production of the ancient play of Pyramus and Thisby. The description, "What hempen homespuns (coarse fellows) have we swaggering here" inspired, in part, the "tree rats" and the "cradle of the Fairy Queen" came to represent for me the mountain and it's magic.

5. *A Midsummer Night's Dream*, Act 3, scene 1, line 1; the woods, Titania is sleeping. Bottom is speaking to the craftsman, setting the stage for their production, making use of the "green plot" as their stage, the "hawthorn brake" (thicket), their "tiring house," (dressing room). In *Mountain Lyrics*, a number of the themes introduced in this

chapter are borrowed. The principal characters are now together on the side of the mountain, the book's "stage," and Mac uses the shrubs as his dressing room. They discuss Jesse's story and their respective roles, and in a manner opposite than that followed by the characters in the play, discuss making something that is not real, real.

6. *A Midsummer Night's Dream*, Act 3, Scene 2, line 250; another part of the woods. In the play confusion reigns. The various plans and attempts to influence the leanings of the heart go far astray. There are anger and threats and some fear, and Puck avoids actual confrontation by ensuring that the adversaries are hopelessly lost from one another. (In this specific verse Lysander is speaking to Demetrius, advising him that neither his threats nor Hermia's weak prayers will deter him from his newfound love of Helena.) The confusion, threats, and fear take a different slant in *Mountain Lyrics*. I didn't attempt to create any love triangles or errant cupid's arrows. The angst and despair goes much deeper with Anna's tragedy and Jesse's troubled past, amidst the confusion of the storm, the haunting presence of the bear and Mac's fateful plans.

7. *A Midsummer Night's Dream*, Act 5, Scene 1, line 375; Athens, the palace of Theseus. The Play of Pyramus and Thisby has just been performed by the craftsmen before Theseus and Hippolyta and others. In this verse the play is over, the actors gone, and Puck is speaking to the audience, referring to the play just ended. The roar of the lion was that which caused Thisby to flee, leaving behind her mantle for Pyramus to find. The moon flees as Pyramus stabs himself,

distraught over what he believes is Thisby's demise. Finally, Thisby, finding Pyramus dead, takes her own life. In *Mountain Lyrics* the events are different. The bear is real, Mac's fate unknown, and Toni despairs, just beginning to grasp what life would be like without Mac.

8. *A Midsummer Night's Dream*, Act 5, Scene 1 lines 303-307; Athens, the palace of Theseus. These words constitute the final words of Pyramus as he expires.

These words are the source of some jest and ridicule in the play and are followed by:

Demetrius. "No die, but an ace, for him; for he is but one."

Lysander. "Less than an ace, man; for his is dead, he is nothing."

Theseus. "With the help of a surgeon he might yet recover, and yet prove an ass."

In *Mountain Lyrics* I attempted to make the words real.

9. *A Midsummer Night's Dream*, Act 3, Scene 2, lines 413-414; Lysander is speaking to himself or the audience about the voice of Puck which has been leading him further into the forest. Lysander and Demetrius are seeking each other to contest their love for Helena. Puck's words, just before this verse are, "Follow my voice. We'll try no manhood (have no test of valor) here." In *Mountain Lyrics*, all the characters are following a number of "voices" the voice of God, Mac, Sister Toni and the mountain itself.

Unlike the suggested confrontations in the play, the tests of valor in *Mountain Lyrics* actually occur.

10. *A Midsummer Night's Dream*, Act 3, Scene 2, line 404; another part of the wood. These are Puck's words to Lysander when he leads Lysander and Demetrius into the woods. "Plainer" is to be read "more level." The phrase seemed an appropriate salutation to the final chapter of the book, whether it is read as calling for a simple, plainer life where we let "the present soak into [us] like water satisfying a long and unquenched thirst," or more literally, hiking off the mountain to more level ground.

AUTHOR'S NOTE

Mountain Lyrics was first inspired by the myths and stories I was lucky enough to learn from my parents. They provided my siblings and me with a multitude of songs and stories that sparked our imaginations and made the world a colorful place.

In addition, I must confess to a life-long fascination with a poem by an unknown author called the Big Rock Candy Mountain. I always hoped to visit a land that was far away, fair, and bright, "Where the handouts grow on bushes and you sleep out every night."

I also was intrigued by the scenes, characters and themes found in Shakespeare's play *A Midsummer Night's Dream*, a story of an ill-fated adventure in the woods.

Finally, I actually discovered a mountain called the Rock Candy Mountain. It rises above the sloping forests and twisting ridgelines that are home to deer, elk and grizzly bears. After a year of procrastination,

I drove into the backcountry and spent a few days and nights on the mountain's slopes and summit. That experience provided the final catalyst for this book.

So I borrowed themes, settings and language, struggled to recall the tales from my childhood, and put together my own story of four days and nights in the woods. Each chapter heading is taken from *A Midsummer Night's Dream*, excerpts that I hope fit well with the content of the chapter that follows.

Near the peak of the Rock Candy Mountain

Mike Connelly lives in Spokane, Washington
with his wife and five kids, two dogs, and two cats.

LaVergne, TN USA
30 April 2010
181215LV00001B/66/P